49

Melting

MAXINE BARRY

Heartline Books

Published by Heartline Books Limited in 2001

First published in the United Kingdom in 2001 by Heartline Books Limited.

Heartline Books Limited
PO Box 22598, London W8 7GB

Heartline Books Ltd. Reg No: 03986653

ISBN 1-903867-22-3

Styled by Oxford Designers & Illustrators

Printed and bound in Great Britain by
Cox & Wyman, Reading, Berkshire

MAXINE BARRY

'Never Say Die' is Maxine Barry's motto. It took five years to get her first book, 'Stolen Fire', published. Someone once told her that the only difference between a published writer and an unpublished one is that the unpublished author gave up!

Maxine, a country girl at heart, lives in a small Oxfordshire village and much of her inspiration comes from the surrounding countryside, and the Oxford Colleges, where she once worked as secretary. A typical Pisces, Maxine is sensitive and creative, which, perhaps, explains why she has always wanted to be a professional writer.

chapter one

Oxford, England

Laurel Van Gilder leaned quickly forward, eagerly craning her slender neck to look out of the taxi window, and get her first good look at Oxford.

The fabled city of dreaming spires.

Her timing was near-perfect. At nearly six o'clock in the evening, the late September sun was just beginning to set, bathing the whole city with that wonderful copper glow that only Autumn could produce. Also, an early fog was just beginning to roll in from the Headington hills, cloaking the famous skyline with a mysterious, atmospheric cloak of clammy mist.

Laurel actually caught her breath. If only she had her video camera with her!

She'd done a fair amount of reading about the city of Oxford on the flight over from Boston, and now she could pick out the stately towers of Christ Church near its green meadow and the domed tops of the Bodleian Old Library and Sheldonian Theatre, all set amid the many crenellated walls of Oxford's numerous, ancient colleges.

'Bit of a picture that, eh love?' the taxi driver's friendly voice suddenly interrupted her thoughts, and she leaned slowly back in her seat, letting out a long, slow breath.

'It sure is.'

Her east-coast American accent was pleasantly deep, and the taxi driver – a forty-something with an appreciative eye – once again glanced in his rear-view mirror. It was not the first time he'd done so on the hour-and-a-half long journey from Heathrow.

'You over here on one of them Rhodes Scholarship things then love?' he fished with casual charm, displaying his one piece of knowledge about the Oxford University system with pride, and giving Laurel a quick smile.

She gave the back of his slightly balding head an amused look.

'No,' she said shortly but sweetly. At twenty-eight, she considered herself a little old to be mistaken for an undergraduate. Not that the taxi driver could be blamed for that. She looked a good five years younger than she actually was as people, especially her more waspish female friends, constantly told her.

The taxi driver's doleful brown eyes once again met her own dark ebony ones in the mirror, and Laurel felt herself relenting a little. What was it about hurt men that made them look so pathetic?

'I've already got my masters,' she explained gently. 'From Radcliffe.'

The name of the prestigious American University meant little to the driver however, who merely shrugged, pulled up at a traffic light, and began to whistle tunelessly through his teeth.

Laurel yawned delicately, but with a gusto that was characteristic of her. 'Are we nearly there yet?' she asked.

The taxi driver quickly shot away from the light, casting a baleful eye at a rather sporty Rover that had pulled up alongside him, and looked set to nab his place.

'Aye? Oh, it was the Woodstock Road you wanted, wasn't it? I dunno love, I dunno this place too well. I'll stop and ask when we get further into the town.'

Laurel shrugged, but never even thought of casting a wary eye at the taxi's ticking meter. When your family was worth multi-millions, taxi fares didn't hold too many terrors!

Other things, however, did.

She felt her slender shoulder blades tense for a moment and she forced them to relax. This was hardly her first trip abroad, she reminded herself angrily. Although it was her first time representing the Van Gilder family on business. The first time as a working member of the clan. And head of the clan, at that…

Always before, Europe had meant holidays to Laurel. Skiing in Austria, buying chocolates in Belgium, shopping for gowns in Paris. In her defence, that had been no more than was expected of her. The Van Gilder heiress had to be seen in all the right spots by the paparazzi, her photographs had to appear in all the right magazines, and her face adorn all the 'in' charity balls. Her father had expected it of her.

Of course, she'd also been expected to have a husband by now. An exiled royal prince perhaps? A famous tycoon, or renowned philanthropist. But so far, her ring finger had remained stubbornly bare, much to her mother's chagrin.

But all those expectations, squabbles and half-hearted plans had stopped, abruptly and horrifically, three short months ago, when her father's limousine on its way to his Boston office, had been rammed by a drunk driver.

Her father, Bernard, had been killed instantly.

Overnight, the Van Gilder empire had trembled. The family unit had threatened to crack. Uncles had hastily come out of the woodwork to 'steady' the stock market and safeguard the family shares. And they had succeeded.

Then there had been the second crisis of the will.

And what a little bombshell that had been!

Laurel felt her shoulder blades begin to ache once

more, a sharp, painful throbbing that left her squirming in her seat. She sighed angrily at herself and began some deep-breathing exercises, forcing her muscles to relax. She was going to have to get used to the responsibilities now weighing on her, she reminded herself grimly.

And this was only the first test. But, really, it was such a simple, easy little thing to do. If she was going to let herself get into such a state over something so…

''Ere, mate, you wouldn't 'appen to know where I can find the Woodstock Road would you?'

The taxi driver's voice once again cut across her reverie, dragging her from the dark path of her thoughts, and she glanced out of the window to see a young man with long, lank hair lean in and cast her a wide-eyed look.

She listened with only half an ear as the stranger, probably a student, gave the driver directions, all the while feasting his eyes on the taxi's passenger. Once they were moving again, she let her mind drift once more.

The Van Gilder family was a large, rich, and influential one. The original Van Gilder, her great-great-great (and was it another great after that?) grandfather, had been a very enterprising Dutchman who'd left his family's diamond company in Amsterdam to set up business in the fledgling United States of America. He'd started off in diamonds, of course, but his sons had gone into railroads. Their sons had gone into ships, and some of the greatest liners of the golden age were Van Gilder babies. Their sons had diverged even further! Nowadays, there were Van Gilders in California making mega-buck movies in Hollywood. Van Gilders in Kansas – corn kings who fed the country and sponsored hospitals. Van Gilders in Canada (lumber barons, naturally) and her own branch of the family, the east-coast Van Gilders. Theirs was perhaps the most divergent of them all. Her father had been a patron of museums, schools and ballets, whilst his company had fingers in pies as diverse as ball bearings, auto-parts, steel, hospital instruments, and educational publishing.

But Bernard Van Gilder had only one child.

Laurel.

But he also had his three younger brothers, and had placed them in charge of his company's many departments. Laurel's uncle, Matthew, knew more about hospital instruments than surgeons but, far more importantly, how to sell them in bulk throughout the world. Uncle Thomas took care of all the hardware, whilst Uncle Craig mopped up the rest. It had been Bernard's job to be the 'patriarch' of the family. Van Gilders had always stood for charity, good works, high profile and, above all, class. And everyone agreed, Bernard had produced one of the classiest families in Massachusetts.

The result was that everyone was happy. The charities prospered and the media had their own 'first family of Boston' to denigrate or praise, according to their current editorial policy. The Van Gilders themselves thrived and enjoyed the fruits of their labours. The reputation of Van Gilder class, elegance, style, that Bernard had worked all his life to safeguard.

And now, Laurel Van Gilder was in charge of the lot.

At least, she thought with a wry twist of her lips, on paper she was. In reality, she was too much of a Van Gilder to believe in her own publicity. Her father had always kept his daughter's feet firmly on the ground.

Her uncles knew more about the running of their respective little mini-empires than she ever would and, like her father before her, she was more than happy to let them continue. She rather loved her uncles, especially Craig, who was her favourite.

Her mother, Mercedes, was a Philadelphia Marsden by birth, and had quickly taken Boston by storm when she'd arrived as a young bride in the sixties. Her parties had the best guests (ex-Presidents abounded), her food was catered for by the impossible-to-book Marcel, her wines came from the best vineyards in France. Her husband had adored her from the very first moment they met, and had continued to do so throughout their thirty-year marriage. The very morning of his death, he'd ordered three dozen pure white roses for his wife, just because she'd bemoaned the fact over the breakfast table that their lavish town rose-garden had no white blooms in it this year.

Bernard Van Gilder's funeral had reflected his status as an all-rounder – a businessman, a patron of the arts, a philanthropist, an old-family, old-fashioned, millionaire.

And now Laurel had been handed the baton, and had no choice but to run with it.

'This is it then love,' the taxi driver chirruped happily. 'What number do you want?'

Laurel hastily took a steadying breath, coming out of her blue funk with something of an effort, and repeated the number of the house she had leased for three months. Once again, she craned her neck to look out of the taxi window, this time to catch her first glimpse of Woodstock Road.

The first thing she noticed were all the trees lined up at the front of all the gardens, creating a 'country avenue' effect. They were mostly cherry trees, she guessed. And she thought about how lovely they must look in spring. The houses themselves were large and individual and, in some mysterious way, utterly British. Nestled in large gardens, they gave way now and then to the odd college or two.

There, on her left, was Green College with the Radcliffe Observatory close by. On her right, a veritable feast of colleges passed by, their windows lit up with twinkling yellow lights, as the sun slid even lower in the sky.

St Annes College was set in so much greenery that the students must feel they had their own park! And, with only the Bevington Road to separate them, there was St Antony's.

She bit her lip as she realised they must have missed the one college that interested her the most – St Bede's.

Oh well! Plenty of time to sight-see later.

The taxi pulled up outside a large, white-painted, villa style house, with a huge magnolia tree in front of it.

'This the place, love?'

'I guess so,' Laurel murmured. Her private secretary had leased the place, site unseen, after learning that Woodstock Road was a suitably prestigious address for her employer.

Laurel reached for the door handle and swung her very long legs out on to the damp pavement. Back home, of course, she usually travelled by limousine, and the chauffeur always opened the doors for her. It was one of the reasons she'd liked holidaying abroad, with her large circle of friends. She got to be 'real' for a few weeks! Living in a rarefied atmosphere might sound good to outsiders, but it could so easily lead you up the garden path if you let it!

Laurel got out and glanced around her, shivering a little in the misty, cool night air. Street lamps were on, giving the long road a rather romantic air. The traffic, for such a big city as Oxford, was surprisingly light.

The taxi driver began grunting as he hauled out the three large suitcases that were stowed in the boot.

Laurel felt the usual slight tinge of guilt. For all her determination not to play the part of madam bountiful, she had to admit she loved clothes. Clothes were her one real vice.

She didn't use the family's credit cards at exclusive jewellery stores. She didn't go to the hairdressers every day, as most of her friends did back home. She didn't go from one holiday resort to another, or have a drug habit, or keep expensive playboys (again like most of her friends back home!).

Her parents, for all their seemingly opulent lifestyles, had always instilled in her the twin evils of taking money for granted and thinking that the world was her playground.

Her only true 'rich-bitch' vice (as she privately thought of it), was her passion for clothes. 'Here, let me take one of those,' she said hastily now, as the taxi driver tried unsuccessfully to juggle the three large cases. She opened the gate leading to the villa, and together they lugged her cases to the small, but charmingly tiled, front porch. A security light had come on as soon as they'd set foot in the garden and, in its welcome light, Laurel took some cash from her Gucci handbag and handed over the fare, together with a very large tip.

The taxi driver beamed at her. In the overhead light, her long, raven-black hair looked eerily (but beautifully) orange. Her sharp cheekbones and the line of her strong jaw had deep shadows playing over them. They made her look like a sexy witch from a Gothic horror movie, the taxi driver thought, with a shiver that had nothing to do with the cold fog. He gave one last lingering sigh at the sight of her, then headed reluctantly back to his cab, to drive his trusty (and rusty) chassis back to Heathrow.

Laurel took the set of keys the estate agent had sent

over to her, and fiddled with the lock. She breathed just a small sigh of relief as the door swung open.

Inside, the central heating timer system had already switched on, and had warmed the place up nicely.

The house was not large by her standards. A quick inspection revealed a charming black-and-white tiled hall with a large, wooden staircase, a pleasant lounge with big bay windows, a fully-equipped kitchen fitted in pine, a music room complete with grand piano, and a conservatory that, unless she'd lost all sense of direction, would catch the early morning sun, and make it the ideal place to have breakfast. Upstairs were three large bedrooms, two with *en suite* bathrooms.

Her mother might find it a bit poky but Laurel thought it would do nicely. Very nicely indeed.

Her own private house, where she could rest her battered soul and catch her breath.

She still missed her father. And the Van Gilder crown still felt so heavy, it gave her a constant headache. But, with typical practicality and pugnacity, she had decided to stay in England for a month or so, and catch up on other UK-related Van Gilder Business.

Her uncles had been only too happy to give her a long list of companies (and company chairmen) to be wined and dined and generally flattered.

At first, she had been a bit resentful. Did they think she was good for nothing else but flying the Van Gilder flag, with her pretty face and elegant style? But then, realistically, she'd quickly acknowledged to herself that that was exactly what her father had done all his life. His handsome face had graced many periodicals, where he'd been photographed shaking the hands of foreign politicians, businessmen and potential allies and rivals alike.

Her uncles might run the companies, but it was her father who had made the contacts, continuously brought in new business, and kept the machine well oiled.

Now everyone was expecting her to do the same.

And she'd die before she let them down!

So, she was here to get on with it. And the first job on the agenda was to oversee and present the prestigious Van Gilder chair award in Psychology, and the Augentine chalice that went with it. The chalice, a fifteenth-century silver example that had somehow escaped the sacking by Henry VIII, had finally found its way into the Van Gilder art collection. It had been a great-uncle of her father who'd first come up with the idea of 'loaning' the chalice to whichever College currently housed the 'Van Gilder' Chair. Which was why it had been shipped to England, and was currently awaiting her phone call to have it transported, under guard, to Oxford. (It was worth, at last insurance valuation, a cool one hundred thousand pounds).

Laurel unpacked in the biggest bedroom and checked out the large, well-appointed bathroom. After a longish flight, a wearying taxi ride, and so much tense introspection, a long hot bath seemed like a good idea.

She quickly ran the hot water, then rifled in one of her suitcases for her toiletries bag and favourite terry-robe. She carried her prizes back to the now steam-filled bathroom and quickly stripped off her plain and simple navy-blue Valentino suit.

She added a generous splash of gardenia and elderflower Chanel bubble bath to the water, which immediately frothed and foamed and began to smell heavenly. Then she quickly stepped out of her plain white underwear, catching a quick glimpse of her naked self in one of the mirrors as she did so.

She was used to what she saw.

At five feet eleven inches tall, she knew most people considered her height both elegant and fashionable. Her slender, even angular curves, were also deemed by most to be the height of feminine beauty. But Laurel tended to think of herself as tall and skinny.

Her long black hair, in her opinion, was just that. Long and black. Others were fascinated by the blue, raven-like quality of her silk-straight locks. Her large ebony eyes were so dark it was almost impossible to make out the round black pupil within them. She'd always believed, ruefully, that they gave her the look of a rather stupid panda.

Others, men especially, found them utterly fascinating.

Her face was angular, as the taxi driver had noticed, and she had very high, pointed cheekbones, a very firm jaw, and a long, straight nose.

Not beautiful.

No. But arresting.

Intriguing.

Fascinating.

Appealing.

Men had been coming up with different adjectives for her triangular face ever since Laurel had hit fifteen. One man had even come up with 'sharp as razors'.

She had almost married him.

He'd been honest. And funny. And, as her father's private investigators had found out, very poor. Laurel wouldn't have cared if he'd been honest about it, but he hadn't. He leased a Lamborghini, conned the use of richer friend's boats, houses, clothes, even jewellery.

All with one aim.

Catching himself a rich heiress!

Laurel winced as she stepped into the too-hot water.

She 'ahhed' and 'eeked' her way down into the tub and finally settled back with a weary sigh. She rather naughtily used one of the bathroom's face flannels to wash off her light make-up, and washed it out guiltily in the bathwater.

Her mother would have had a hissing fit. But Laurel seldom wore much make-up in the daytime anyway. Like a lot of raven-haired women, her skin was naturally very pale and she rather liked the white-faced look, and so wore very little by way of foundation and blusher. Her large dark eyes would look ridiculous with lashes of mascara. By far the greatest amount of money she spent on make-up was on the purchase of lipstick.

Laurel had a rather big mouth – both literally and figuratively. Literally, her full lips looked stunning when painted virtually any colour. Figuratively, her tendency to say what she thought had got her in more trouble over the years than her wealth, looks and somewhat lavish sense of humour combined.

Now she shrugged off her past sins and pushed them firmly behind her.

After all, she told herself firmly, there was nothing to be gained by dwelling on the past. Her father was gone, and she'd just have to get used to it. She had loved him deeply. He'd been kind and generous, as well as sophisticated and clever. The shock of his sudden loss had been terrific, as had the anger at the waste and stupidity of it.

But that, too, had now deadened from a roaring, raging agony to a dull and deadening ache.

Her father would have been the first to tell her to stop moping and pull her finger out. His will had made it plain that she was to carry on in his stead. He'd left all his money, his company shares, and his power, to her.

Her uncles got to keep everything they had had under

Bernard's benevolent leadership. Their titles, huge salaries, and many other benefits. But it had been made well and truly clear to everyone, that Laurel was now the head of the family.

And she was up to it. She had to be.

Her fiancé and his treachery had all but faded from her memory now. She'd been eighteen, and she'd well and truly had her feathers singed but they'd all grown back again.

She was here in Oxford to award the prestigious (and lucrative) Van Gilder Chair to its worthy winner and present the chalice to his or her college for the duration, and then to fly the Van Gilder flag at its UK affiliates.

A nice and easy introduction. Her father could have done it standing on his head.

Nothing to it. She was fine. Everything was fine.

Laurel suddenly felt tears running down her face. They took her by surprise and she sat up with a jerk, raising a hand to her cheeks and then staring at her salt-dampened fingers in astonishment. 'Damn!' she said angrily.

'Oh Damn!'

Grimly, she set about washing her hair, then scrubbing her face and body with a lavishly-expensive cream soap. Afterwards she towelled herself dry, wrapped her long hair in a towel (it might look good, but it took ages to dry!) and marched determinedly downstairs.

The agents had stocked the cupboards well and, on impulse, she made herself a mug of Horlicks, something she hadn't drunk in years. Finally, feeling faintly little-girl-ridiculous, she moved into the living room and put on the television, blinked at the absence of hard-sell advertising, realised she was watching the BBC and settled back on her sofa.

Sometimes, life was hell.

The first thing Laurel did the next morning was explore. She was in a new city and, as usual, there was just too much to see.

She took a taxi into the centre of town, and by the time she'd alighted at the Martyr's Memorial, she had already made a mental note to buy herself a bicycle for Oxford was riddled with them.

Students in black 'subfusc' cycled to their colleges to take part in the Matriculation Ceremony, and have their first year photograph taken. Housewives cycled to work. Dons cycled to schools, or clubs, or pubs, or the Ashmolean Museum. Old ladies cycled. Women with babies strapped to their backs cycled.

And Laurel Van Gilder would cycle too.

Her first stop was Christ Church. Oxford was the only city she had heard of, where its cathedral was in the middle of a college, and she was intrigued by the thought of it.

She listened to a choir practising for hours, then walked in the meadow and tried to see some deer. They either weren't around that day (she saw lots of cows however) or else she had her colleges mixed up, and it was Magdalen College that had the deer. Then she found Broad Street and got lost (quite literally) amid the maze of shelves in the famous Blackwells bookshop. She had elevenses at a Christian coffee shop in St Aldates, explored the wonderful arches and narrow lanes around Wadham College, stumbled into a smelly but intriguing 'covered market' off Cornmarket street, and then lunched at Browns.

Her feet ached, her eyes feasted on ancient British architecture, and her soul began to heal in the waning September sun.

That afternoon, she indulged herself with a wonderful stroll through the Botanical gardens, watched the mechanical figures come out as the Carfax clock struck four, and after taking a taxi to the suburb of Botley, she bought herself the promised bicycle.

It was brand new, a pretty and ostentatious shade of cherry-pink, big, lightweight and wonderful to ride. It also had so many gears on it that she wondered if she should have taken lessons before buying it.

Although the Woodstock Road was a long way from Botley, Laurel brought a street map from the bicycle shop and headed determinedly for home.

She was wearing her Calvin Klein faded blue jeans, a warm and chunky Arran sweater in lovely tones of beige, orange, and chocolate brown, and a heavy gold chain that caught the light of the sun and threw up gold reflections on the underside of her chin and neck. Her long, black hair was held back off her face by an impromptu pony-tail, but wisps tended to keep coming free and fall in her eyes.

The bright sunlight was beginning to fade by the time she reached St Giles, and pedalled past St Cross College and the Oriental Institute.

Her legs were aching pleasantly from the unaccustomed exercise and pigeons fluttered on to the college roofs around her. The worst of the rush-hour traffic was behind her, but she still enjoyed cycling in and out of the queues of traffic stuck at the lights, pitying the drivers trapped in their stuffy cars.

She felt, for some reason she couldn't quite define, inordinately better. No longer the haunted, lonely, sorry-for-herself girl who'd surprised herself by crying last night. She was suddenly young, wealthy, free, not too ugly, and in a wonderful new city.

She was also not paying attention to that wonderful new city's rules of the road!

Like all Americans newly arrived in Britain, she had her mind set on right-hand drive. In the States, as in most other European countries, traffic drove on the right. In England, however, they drove on the left.

It had been very strange at first, riding (or, to be more accurate, wobbling) away from the bicycle shop, and she'd had to force herself to concentrate on what she was doing.

Cars approached her from the right. Come to a T-junction, and you had to look right.

At first, the very newness of it had kept her alert. All the way from Botley she'd been very conscious of the fact that she was riding along on, what felt to her, like the wrong side of the road.

By the time she'd got to the centre of town, however, the novelty had begun to wear off. She'd begun to relax and enjoy the new experience of riding a bike along Oxford's lovely streets. And it had made her careless.

As she approached the college, she had decided to leave the exploring of St Bedes until last, but now she glanced at her watch. Too late now to really do it justice. Best wait until tomorrow and then give it an impromptu once over. If she told them she was coming, she'd get the red carpet treatment, and that was the last thing she wanted.

As she approached it, she glanced at the pale cream Cotswold stone walls and the ancient, mullioned windows.

She didn't see the low, green, open-topped Morgan that was cruising along, perfectly legally, in front of her.

She knew there was a street up ahead where she could turn off, to ride up Walton Street. It was a longer route home, but she was in no hurry.

She glanced automatically to her right.

Nothing coming, all was clear.

She turned left. Straight into the side of the Morgan!

Laurel just had time to give a loud yelp of fright, and see a silver-white head turn to look, startled, in her direction. For a fraction of a second, she caught a flash of amazingly light, electric-blue eyes.

Then there was the weird sensation of flight as her bike hit the car, catapulting her slight frame into the air and over the bonnet of the sports car.

In her ears, the squeal of the Morgan's brake sounded hideously loud and ominous.

She had, in fact, just enough time to imagine the headlines in the papers back home – 'Van Gilder Heiress Killed in Tragic Oxford Car Crash'. More distressingly, she had just a moment left to think about how much hitting the pavement was going to hurt. And then she saw the paving stones rushing up at her face. She felt her left shoulder hit the ground, a painful jolting blow, before a sharp pain lanced through her head.

Blackness rushed up to claim her.

chapter two

Professor Gideon Welles, a well-respected Fellow of St Bedes and Don in Experimental Psychology, rammed on the brakes of his low-slung Morgan.

His heart shot into his throat and seemed to lodge there.

He saw the woman cyclist catapult over the bonnet of his car in a sick kind of daze. Everything happened so fast, he couldn't think in his usual stream of consciousness. Just in bare flickers of awareness.

He had a fleeting impression of long dark hair, wrapping itself around a pale, oval face.

He caught a glimpse of colour – the knitted jumper she was wearing.

He could hear the high-pitched squeal of his brakes as the car obediently snapped to a halt, and felt the pressure of the seat-belt suddenly tighten across his chest.

And then, a sudden silence.

The woman had disappeared but he knew, with the one part of his brain that was still coldly rational, that she had not gone far. Only as far as the pavement, in fact.

For what felt like years, but was really only a second, he sat numbly in the car before leaping into action. He quickly dealt with his seat-belt, found the release mechanism, and snapped it open.

Just then, a large woman, walking out from the entrance of Little Clarendon Street, stopped in the middle of the road, her mouth falling comically open.

Gideon realised the engine of his car was still running, and he quickly turned it off. Even in a crisis, Professor

Welles was a cool operator. He opened the door of the sports car as the woman bystander dropped her shopping bag and began to waddle anxiously towards the young girl lying sprawled on the pavement.

Gideon was already getting out of the car. It was always a sight that tickled his students, because the Morgan was so low-slung and Gideon Welles easily topped six feet five inches. But usually he was the picture of unexpected grace. This time, however, he looked a bit like a puppet with one string broken!

He could feel that his movements were uncoordinated, jerky even, and knew, with his knowledge of both medicine and the workings of the human mind, that it was the effects of shock rippling through his system.

He easily recognised all the signs – the numbness, the sensation of 'watching it all happen from a distance', the cold, sick feeling in the pit of his stomach that made him want to heave.

None of these feelings showed on his face, however, as he walked quickly around the side of the classic green sports car and moved rapidly towards the woman on the pavement.

His eyes instantly sought her face.

Her eyes were closed. Her skin a whiter shade of pale.

There was no blood on her face though, no outward sign of injury and his eyes dropped quickly to her chest.

Below the expensive jersey, her chest rose and fell rhythmically, and it was only then that he let out a long, shaken sigh. She was not dead. That was all that mattered.

'What happened?'

The large woman was hovering over the stricken figure of Laurel Van Gilder, moving nervously from one foot to the other, not sure what she ought to be doing. 'Did she faint?'

Gideon ignored her, and instead folded his very long frame into a crouching position over the unconscious figure. He checked her pulse first, and was relieved to find it strong and steady, if a little fast.

Then he reached into the passenger side of his Morgan for a mobile phone, and quickly dialled for an ambulance.

By now, the large woman was not alone in studying the prone, pale and inert figure on the pavement. A postman, delivering his final mail of the day, had pulled up in his van and, ever-practical, pulled the mangled cherry-pink bike, which had been lying half under the wheels of the Morgan, on to one side, out of the way of other traffic. A few others – pedestrians who'd been using the same pavement – began to congregate around Laurel, their natural curiosity liberally laced with genuine concern.

'Poor thing,' some old lady muttered. 'Crashed her bike, I expect.'

There was a general murmur. With so many people riding bicycles, people were bound to have accidents.

Gideon gave the ambulance service their precise location, and turned off the phone. His voice was cool, clear, and gave no indication of the true state of his rather frayed nerves.

He returned to the dark-haired, unconscious woman, and shrugged off his heavy suede jacket. He carefully laid it over her, checked that her air passages were clear, and leaned back on his heels.

Only then, when everything was done, taken care of and seen to, did he look at her properly.

She looked gauntly beautiful. Her face seemed all sexy sharp angles – high cheekbones, a long, well-defined nose, and a determined jaw. Looking so pale, and lying so still, she looked half-dead.

His heartbeat began to slow to a more normal pace as he continued to watch her regular breathing, and his own face, which had been ashen, began to take on a more normal hue.

A police car arrived. Someone had thought to phone them, although Gideon himself had thought only of the ambulance. The possible consequences to himself of this accident hadn't even crossed his mind.

The two officers were young, but very competent. Within moments, they'd found witnesses to the accident – one, a woman who'd been driving behind Gideon and had pulled up, shaken, a few yards along the road. She willingly confirmed that the car in front of her hadn't been speeding, and that the cyclist had simply ridden straight into him.

Another witness, a student crossing the churchyard opposite the scene, confirmed this version of events, and had already given a clear-cut account of the incident when the ambulance arrived.

The paramedics deftly checked their patient for broken bones, and talked in professional detachment about her 'head injury'. Gideon watched them transfer her onto the stretcher, relief pouring over him that, at last, things were being done and he went to follow them automatically. But one of the policemen, with a very gentle but firm grip of his arm, pulled him back.

The next few hours passed very quickly. But when he later looked back on them, they seemed like the longest of his life.

First of all, he was breathalysed on the spot, an oddly humiliating experience even though the purely rational part of his brain told him it was only fair. The police were only doing their job, and there was absolutely nothing personal in it. Nobody had even so much as hinted that he might be drunk or irresponsible. Even so, as he breathed into the plastic belt he felt a surge of resentment.

By then, he'd given his details to the authorities, and nobody was very much surprised when Professor Gideon Welles checked out as having no alcohol in his bloodstream whatsoever.

In the sometimes wary world of town versus gown, the civilian population of Oxford had a love-hate relationship with the academics living amongst their midst. Drunken students could be a pest. Liberal-minded, banner-waving radical Dons could be an embarrassment. Generally, though, the police had a cautious respect for the members of Oxford's many colleges. The University was, after all, one of the best in the world and it did bestow on the city of Oxford some very real privileges. So, after signing his statement, he was allowed to collect his Morgan from the police car park and leave without any more formalities.

Gideon barely registered the slight dent on the car's right-hand fender that was scraped and smeared with a bright, incongruous cherry-pink. Normally, the slightest scratch on his prized possession would have been one of the few things that could rouse him to any serious display of anger. Now, he barely gave it a frowning look before folding in his long length behind the wheel.

When he'd first bought the car, he'd had to have a mechanic reposition the seat right back in the car's body in order to accommodate his long legs. All his friends had laughingly told him that he looked like a stork trying to get into a length of pipe whenever he drove the car, but his Morgan was one of the few luxuries he had ever wanted.

And, as a general rule, Gideon Welles was used to getting what he wanted.

He drove straight to the John Radcliffe Hospital in Headington. By now it was fully dark and getting late, but he needed to know for himself how she was doing.

When he arrived, he had a terrible time finding her. The police had not told him her name, and so he was forced to hang around the huge reception area whilst they tried to trace his unknown accident victim. Eventually he was told she was in a ward on the sixth floor. The receptionist, naturally, could give no details as to her condition or prognosis.

The police, too, had given him no indication of her condition, probably because they had not known it. Instead, their dry and precise explanations of the law had had to take precedence, although he'd been assured there were unlikely to be any charges because of the witnesses and their own expert crash reconstruction skills. He'd obviously not been drunk, had not been speeding, and had not been driving in a reckless manner likely to cause injury.

It had been a relief, of course, but it had never been his primary concern. Now, as he made his way to the lifts, he felt the tension begin to rebuild in his shoulders. He'd never been responsible for hurting anyone before, and the fact that it had been purely accidental wasn't really helping.

At the lifts, two women, each holding big bouquets of flowers, glanced at him as he stood silently beside them.

They had to look a long way up! One woman, middle-aged and rounding out a little in the middle, glanced across at her companion, a much younger and leaner version of herself. Obviously mother and daughter.

The mother's lips twitched at the openly interested look in her daughter's eyes.

Not that she could blame her. She'd always liked tall

men herself, and this one towered above them both. And his colouring was so striking too. His hair was almost white, but not the white of an old man. No, this had sort of old-gold tints in it and was thick and well-cut, exposing shapely ears, a high forehead, and tapered to a duck's tale in the nape of his neck.

At the moment he was staring straight ahead. Both mother and daughter, from opposite sides of him, stared at a classical profile. His eyebrows, of the same old-gold colour, met over eyes that were…

The door to the lift 'pinged' open, and both women quickly moved forward.

Gideon politely stood to one side to let the ladies in first, and as they both turned inside the large square lift, they were at last left facing him head on.

The older of the women audibly gasped. She'd been half expecting blue eyes, of course, to go with the man's colouring, but not eyes *that* blue!

Her daughter gave her a quick, half-angry, half-amused look.

Her mother began to blush like a schoolgirl.

Gideon, noticing none of this, simply stepped inside, turned, and then glanced down to the younger woman.

'Which floor would you like ladies?'

The daughter, who'd been busy giving her mother a 'please don't embarrass me' look, suddenly jerked into life and stared up at him. And gasped herself.

It was one thing to maintain a dignified distance when contemplating a stranger who stood a few feet away. It was totally another thing to find a gorgeous giant, looking down at you with eyes that seemed to glow like neon blue lights.

'What floor would you ladies like?' he asked politely.

'Five please,' the mother said primly, regaining lost

ground and having recovered her dignity sufficiently to give her daughter a silent 'behave' look.

Gideon half-smiled in an automatic gesture, and pressed buttons five and six.

Behind his back, mother and daughter exchanged meaningful glances. Both of them were grinning in companionable kinship when they left the lift.

Gideon took a deep breath as the lift climbed to the last floor. He was prepared for the worst.

But, once again, the more coldly clinical side of his brain told him to expect the best. The woman had been breathing well. Her pulse had been strong. The paramedics had found no broken bones, and the 'head injury' most likely meant a straightforward concussion rather than serious brain damage.

But the deeply human side of him persisted in being terrified. What if she did develop a blood clot and die? Or if she was left permanently mentally disabled?

His palms were sweating as he approached the nurses station, and he had to surreptitiously clear his suddenly dry throat.

Once again, none of his turmoil showed on his face.

Nurse Clare Fielding looked up to see a man striding confidently towards her. He was dressed casually but very well, in grey slacks and a black jersey. His black suede jacket was still at the police station, where he'd forgotten to claim it.

'Good evening,' Gideon, once again, automatically half-smiled. A smile was the easiest and simplest way of displaying non-aggression and was a regular, unconscious gesture of his.

He had no way of knowing what it did to the women who were witnesses to it.

Clare felt herself react, even before she realised it. Her

breathing quickened. Her whole body seemed to snap to a sort of instinctive sexual attention.

At five feet four, and rather rounded at the hips and breast, she suddenly felt like a rather ugly duckling in the presence of a swan. There was something about the man that practically oozed elegance. Perhaps it was the fact that he was so lean as well as tall, but with the leanness of hard muscle about the chest and arms.

Perhaps it was his colouring – so silvery-fair.

Perhaps it was the voice. Those two simple words had been spoken with a classical Oxford precision, and in a deep-timbered tone that made her toenails curl.

Perhaps it was the clothes – casually elegant, off-hand expensive. Whatever. It had certainly brightened up a rather dull, routine night shift!

'I was told you have a patient here. She had an accident on her bicycle on the Woodstock Road, about six-thirty this evening?'

Clare knew instantly who he meant. 'Oh yes. A woman, about twenty years of age. Long black hair?'

Gideon nodded. 'Yes. Can you tell me how she's doing?'

Clare's eyes suddenly focussed into a more professional curiosity. So far, they had no name to go with the victim. Unlike car-crash victims who had driver's licences with them, and other numerous means of identification, casual bike riders were sometimes brought in with no identification on them at all.

Such was the case with the patient in 4B. Her clothes, like this man's, had been casual but expensive. She had a receipt for the bicycle she'd been riding in the pocket of her jeans but, since she'd paid in cash, the bicycle shop had been unable to supply them with a name from a cheque or bank card.

The police probably had better things to do than trace her. She would no doubt be able to give them all the details they needed for their respective paperwork when she woke up in the morning.

'Do you know her?' the nurse asked abruptly. 'I mean,' she amended hastily, 'are you a relative?'

Gideon shook his head. 'No. Mine was the car she collided with.'

'Oh.'

He watched the nurse's eyes, a rather expressive hazel in colour, suddenly darken. As a psychologist, he could easily read her body language. Heading it off, he calmly explained what had happened – emphasising that he wasn't to blame and that the police were pressing no charges. He ended with a frank admission that he was worried she might be seriously injured.

Seeing that she still hesitated, he quickly offered her some identification of his own. Learning that he was a Fellow of St Bedes, a respected Oxford Don and a pillar of the community, the last of Clare's barriers finally broke down.

'Well, strictly speaking, the patient shouldn't have visitors who aren't relatives,' she began, giving a quick and guilty look over her shoulder.

Gideon already knew that. 'She hasn't had anyone come and see her before now?' he asked, somewhat surprised.

Clare shook her head. 'We don't even know who she is, I'm afraid,' she admitted, more openly than the Matron would have approved of.

Gideon shook his head slowly. He hadn't expected this complication. 'But you can tell me how she's doing?' he asked, allowing his voice to drop an octave. 'I mean, she is going to make a full recovery?' he gently persisted.

He wondered, ruefully, what his own therapist would have said about him only now asking that question. It had, after all, been all that he'd really wanted to know.

It had been compulsory for him to spend three years in therapy with a fully-qualified psychiatrist, as part of his own academic studies. As a BA, MA, and with a Ph.D. in Experimental Psychology, it was only common sense (and law!) to have himself thoroughly analysed before being given a licence to practice psychology on the general public.

Not that he'd ever really intended to take on patients. Right from the start, he'd had his sights set firmly on a teaching career. And, since he always reached for the best, a post at an Oxford College had been the logical goal.

One that he'd achieved before reaching the age of thirty.

Clare Fielding, realising the poor man must be on tenterhooks no matter how well he hid it, suddenly gave him a bright, sympathetic smile. 'Oh yes, she'll be fine,' she reassured him. 'She was X-rayed the moment she was brought in, and seen by a neurologist. It's a simple straightforward concussion. Very slight. I think she'll probably be released tomorrow, once the doctor's seen her again and spoken to her. We have to make sure there's no loss of memory, or any speech problems, you see. Of course, ideally, she should be kept in for observation, but what with the bed shortage being like it is…'

Clare suddenly realised she was babbling and quickly shut up. But it was those eyes that were doing it. Watching her so steadily. Burning like blue flames right into her deepest, darkest, most private…

She took a shaky breath.

Those eyes should definitely carry a public health

warning, she thought ruefully. Then, with a sinking heart, she noticed the Sister just leaving the ward at the end of the corridor.

'Look, I'll have a word with the Sister,' Clare offered bravely. 'She might just let you pop in to see her. You know, just to put your mind at rest…'

But don't hold your breath, she thought silently.

But Sister Jenkinson had heard of him. Apparently, her niece had been one of his students several years ago. She was now, she proudly informed him, a psychiatrist in private practice, making a lot of money.

Gideon, who had a phenomenal memory, was able to give the Sister a rather flattering amount of information about her niece's academic prowess. And so it was that, against all the rules, when Laurel Van Gilder struggled towards consciousness some nine hours later, Professor Gideon Welles was sat by her bedside.

Laurel came to slowly, wondering why it was so hard to open her eyes. They felt almost glued together.

Usually she awoke instantly, with an alertness and good humour that was envied by poorer risers.

Today, even before she was aware, even before she had opened her eyes, she knew that something was not quite right. After several tries, she eventually forced her eyelids apart and blinked.

Her first sensation was of whiteness. Then of movement.

Sound. Rattling cups, cheerful voices…

What on earth?

She made to jerk upright, then wished she hadn't, as her head began to throb warningly.

'You'd better lie still.'

That voice was much closer than the other background noise. Her head turned in its direction, fast at first, and then, as her poor aching head protested, much, much slower.

She felt as though she had the worst hangover ever recorded. Had she got drunk last night? Laurel had been eighteen when she'd first got drunk. On champagne, at one of her cousin's weddings. She'd vowed never to again.

Then, as her head continued to turn in the direction of the voice, she noticed other things. An old woman in a bed opposite her, a bottle of Lemon Barley water standing on a tray that was positioned over her thin legs.

She noticed a vase of flowers on the small bedside cabinet beside her.

And, suddenly, she joined all the dots together.

Hospital. She was waking up in a hospital.

Then she remembered a flash of green. The squeal of brakes.

Her bike! Oh no, she'd crashed her new bike!

'Damn,' she said venomously, in an unladylike, but very honest, reaction.

That voice again. Amused now. And yet angry.

Her head turned the rest of the way. And her large black eyes widened even further.

Sat beside her was a silver vision. Some incredible spirit of ancient fable, or an alien. Then she realised that it was only the sunlight, streaming through the cracks in the Venetian blinds that covered the windows, that were playing such hideous tricks on her.

It was a only a man who sat beside her. One slat had allowed light to shine in a vertical channel right across the top of the man's head, making his very fair hair shine almost painfully bright.

Another vertical slat fell right across his eyes. It illuminated the fair brows and the bright, startlingly electric-blue eyes, turning him into a fantastic looking figure. Then he leaned slightly forward on the chair, and his whole face emerged into the normal light.

And Laurel found herself face-to-face with the most handsome man she'd ever seen!

Two things happened at once. She remembered flying over the bonnet of a green car, and the brief glimpse of white hair and electric-blue eyes.

And her head began to hurt in earnest.

She put a hand up to her temple, then leaned back against the pillow with a small groan.

'Oh damn,' she said again, this time more weakly, more wearily. It was her favourite swear word – not as vulgar as some, not as tame as others. When she'd been growing up, her father had chastised her severely for using it, which was probably why it had been such a favourite.

Now, though, it seemed to sum up the state of her life to perfection.

'Do you feel all right?'

The moment he said it, Gideon could have kicked himself. And when the woman turned those huge, black, expressive eyes in his direction, a look of half-sneering, half-exasperated frustration on her face, he was already aware of having set himself up for it.

'Do I look all right?' Laurel snapped.

'No. But then, if you will go around flinging your bike under sports cars, you can't expect to, can you?'

Once again, the moment he said it, he wished he hadn't.

Of course, the psychologist in him knew why he was so angry and so totally lacking in sympathy.

All night long, he'd sat here, watching her sleep. At first, he'd felt only relief. It was a mild concussion after all. She'd be all right, there was no harm done, nobody's life had ended. Then the relief had, classically, given way to guilt and then anger. Guilt that he hadn't been using his mirrors more. Hadn't been paying proper attention. Guilt had convinced him that he should have been able to second guess her. Should have known what was about to happen.

But no human being had the gift of foresight, and so that unreasonable sensation of guilt had transformed itself into anger.

Just what had she thought she was doing, scaring him like that? Not to mention leaving a hideous, cherry-pink scratch on his precious car!

Of course, he hadn't planned on giving way to any of his anger. In fact, in his mind, he'd played over this scene a hundred times in the night.

She'd wake up.

He'd reassure her that all was well. Kindly explain to her exactly what had happened. Get names off her of her nearest and dearest, and assure her that he'd phone them and get them over here. He'd frankly tell her who he was and how the accident had happened, being very sensitive to her feelings, and lightly skating over the fact that it was all her fault.

She'd be grateful and appreciative, he'd buy her some flowers from the shop on the first floor, and then he'd leave, never having to set eyes on her again.

Now he found himself trading insults with her in the first few minutes. He took a calming, warning breath. Cool down, he ordered himself. Don't let her rattle you!

Laurel could hardly believe her ears. What was he saying to her? Of all the pig-headed, insensitive louts.

'What? What do you mean?' she squeaked, indignation making her huff and puff like a fish out of water.

'Do I always ride my bike into cars? Of course I don't. Do you always run over cyclists? I seem to remember that was some fancy sports car you had,' she accused, her voice sharpening into its more confident, loud tone. 'You were speeding, I suppose,' she finished, just for good measure.

She watched, suddenly speechless, as a tide of red spread across his face and then receded. She'd never seen such a rapid colour change in a man before.

He really was most extraordinary…

Belatedly, she began to notice details. The very fine quality of his skin – so fair and so British. The scent coming off him – aftershave that smelled of forests but mixed with a more natural aroma that was musky and totally male. Suddenly she noticed the creases in his clothes, the tired lines around his very lovely mouth, the deep grooves in his quite wonderful cheeks.

'You've been here all night,' she said abruptly. It came out more like an accusation.

Gideon felt his own lips turn into a sneer now.

Accusing him of speeding! She was the one who'd ran into him. Literally! Of all the damned nerve!

'Yes. Silly of me, wasn't it, but I actually wanted to make sure you were all right,' he snapped back icily. 'I was worried that you would wake up alone and frightened.'

Hah, he added mentally. As if! If she woke up alone in the midst of a wolf-pack, it would be the wolves that ran off howling.

'Oh,' Laurel said meekly, the wind taken well and truly out of her sails.

'You're an American, I take it,' Gideon said. Her accent had been one of the first things he noticed about her. Trust him to get saddled with a kamikaze

American female. She was probably neurotic as well.

'Yes. I got here yesterday. No. It must be...two days?'

Her black, well-shaped brows creased into a frown as she fought a sudden sensation of panic. 'How long have I been here?' she snapped, fear making her sharp as she began to wonder what kind of damage had been done.

Had the Press got hold of it? Had anyone told her mother? Hell, she hoped not. She could just imagine her telling all her uncles that she wasn't up to this.

'You've been here overnight,' Gideon said coldly, unused to being spoken to like this.

He was used to being looked up to. Both literally and figuratively. He was Professor Welles. The youngest ever man to be given a full Fellowship of St Bedes. Professor Welles, who was sought after, courted, fêted, and wooed by other Universities to give lectures and attend their conferences. He was chased by journalists to go on their radio shows and write articles for their prestigious publications.

And here was this loud-mouthed American female, demanding answers and looking at him as if it was all his fault.

'Damn it, woman, you rode into me,' he snapped.

Laurel, who'd been having nightmare visions of being called back to Boston in disgrace, her first-ever overseas visit as a Van Gilder ambassador ending in an ignominious shambles, suddenly looked at him blankly.

'Huh?'

'The accident,' he snapped. 'You ran into me. What did you think you were doing, just turning into me like that without even looking?'

And, suddenly, with those angry words, Laurel remembered the rest of it. She'd been looking left, when she should have been looking right. Or was it the other way around?

She rubbed her aching head wearily.

'I'm sorry,' she said simply. 'You're quite right,' she admitted, 'it was all my fault.'

But Gideon, who would normally have been the first to recognise her honesty and graciously accept the apology, was in no mood to be the perfect gentleman today.

'I know it was. But that didn't stop me from being hauled off to the police station in front of witnesses and having to blow into a stupid plastic bag.'

His voice was icy. Frigidly cold and clipped, but quiet.

'Well, excuse me for breathing,' she drawled sardonically. 'It was only a breathalyser test, for crying out loud,' she drawled. 'Get over it!'

What was it with this guy?

Gideon slowly got to his feet.

Laurel watched him get up…and up…and up. Sheesh! How tall was he?

'It might be all in a day's work for you, madam,' Gideon said through gritted teeth. 'But I, for one, don't take run ins with the police lightly. Now, since you're obviously fully recovered,' his lips twitched grimly, 'I'll bid you good day.'

Laurel was aware of two things simultaneously. One, that he really was very upset about the breathalyser thing. And two, he was furiously angry but acting like he was having a day out in the country. It was like he couldn't even lose his temper properly. For the first time, Laurel realised he hadn't even raised his voice.

As he stood towering over her, her eyes widened as she interpreted the look in his. His eyes were the colour of a glacier now – a sort of silvery-grey azure.

Everything about him radiated cold, masculine superiority.

What an iceman, she thought.

And her heart seemed to do a weird kind of jig under her ribcage. As he stalked away, she thanked her lucky stars that she was never going to have to see him again.

He'd probably freeze her to death!

chapter three

Laurel gave herself one last check in the full-length mirror. She was wearing an original by Valentino, a stunning flame-orange creation that fell in luminous flowing hues of gold, orange, red and bronze to her feet.

The dress had straps that tied at the nape of her neck, and widened out into two swathes of material that criss-crossed her breasts, leaving her shoulders, arms, and most of her ribcage bare. The dress met at a tapering point in the small of her back, before falling into a dead-straight line to her ankles. The material was of the finest silk, and glimmered, shimmered, and glowed like flames as she moved.

It was, perhaps, rather racy for a fuddy-duddy Oxford college dinner, but Laurel wasn't going to worry about it too much. Surely, in this day and age, even an Oxford college – that bastion of male privilege – would have been dragged a little way into the twenty-first century?

Her long black hair had presented a bit of problem – left loose it would fall to the middle of her back, and would undoubtedly be a wonderful contrast against her bare skin and bright silk. Unfortunately, left loose, long hair also made her look like a sixteen-year-old.

On the other hand, she didn't particularly want to put it up. Long, elegant, complicated chignons looked wonderful, but they were impossible to relax in. She'd always be worried about the hairdresser's 'invisible' pins coming out and unrolling her coils of hair, just as she was about to start the soup course.

In the end she compromised, and asked for it to be pulled severely back off her face, giving the hairdresser *carte blanche* with a French pleat.

It had, perhaps, been tempting fate a bit to tell the rather effete young man that the hair salon had sent around, to 'go wild' with the pleat. Because, of course, he had.

Laurel had had a long string of amber and silver beads on her dressing table and the hairdresser, eyeing the flame-coloured Valentino hanging ready on the front of her wardrobe door, had persuaded her to let him use the beads in her hair.

Now, glinting amongst the neat, intricate French pleat, were glittering sparkles of silver and amber, a wonderful contrast against the dark raven of her hair.

With her five foot eleven inch slender length pushed up to over six feet by her silver high-heeled shoes, she looked much more glamorous and 'showy' than she had really intended.

She gazed at the mirror with a small scowl.

She wore very little make-up, preferring to leave her rather pale complexion well enough alone. Just a touch of lipstick, a fairly neutral colour, and she looked, well, a bit like a tarted-up beanpole, she thought ruefully.

She heard the sound of the taxi outside, and quickly gathered up her silver evening bag and a plain black cape, and hurried outside for the short drive to the college.

She was met at the front gate of St Bedes, or 'The Venerable' as most people referred to the college, by its current Principle, Lord St John James.

'My dear, so glad you could come,' he greeted her effusively, opening the taxi door for her.

'Please call me Sin-Jun, everyone does.'

It took Laurel a startled moment to realise that this was

how the British pronounced St John. Then she smiled her thanks and murmured a greeting, letting him help her out of the taxi, and pretending not to notice that Lord St John James was trying not to look down the front of her dress.

'It's my honour to be here, Lord, er, Sin-Jun,' she murmured.

He was a tall, military-looking man, with eyes that saw everything and he sported a very dashing moustache. He was the kind of man who would probably have made women of her grandmother's generation swoon.

As it was, Laurel found him touchingly sweet.

As he politely demurred and began leading her through the grounds, she listened to his very practised urbane conversation with a growing affection. Old-fashioned gentlemen were hard to come by, and if you couldn't find them in a Oxford college, where would you?

'You'll be glad to know that the Augentine chalice arrived this afternoon,' Sin-Jun carried on. 'I have arranged for it to be displayed in a locked glass-fronted cabinet in the hall in front of the Senior Common Room at the appropriate time. Until then, of course, it's strictly hush-hush,' he assured her.

Officially, no one was supposed to know who had been awarded the Van Gilder chair until Laurel herself announced it. But, due to practicalities, it was necessary to inform the proper College authority in advance, in order for them to make appropriate preparations.

'Thank you,' Laurel said gratefully.

Because it went dark early in the Michaelmas Term, she wasn't able to see much of the gardens, but all the buildings were cheerfully lit up, the security lights highlighting the crenellated walls and the ancient architecture.

As they approached the Senior common room, where

the Fellows of the college relaxed and socialised, Lord St John James had already explained to her a little about the college and Oxford University as a whole.

Some of it she knew already. For instance, there wasn't, strictly speaking, a 'University' building at all. Oxford had over thirty colleges that collectively made up the University, along with such other august institutions as the Ruskin School, the Bodleian, several museums and even the University Press.

As Laurel listened with genuine interest to Lord St John's brief résumé of St Bedes, she began to actively look forward to the evening.

Although she was there simply to hand over the Van Gilder chair in Psychology to the winner, she began, for the first time, to really appreciate its true significance.

The Chair was for three years, and was awarded to a Fellow or Research Fellow of an Oxford college who had done the most to advance the field of Psychology. It also carried with it a substantial annual income and was, therefore, most sought after.

With the money that came with the Chair, learned tomes could be written by the recipient, simply because it freed his or her time to devote themselves purely to academic research. Which explained, Laurel thought wryly, why Sin-Jun was being (for an Englishman) so gushingly fulsome in his welcome!

The Principal lead the way across a large entrance hall where a large glass-fronted cabinet already held a plethora of sporting cups and academic awards, and approached a set of double green baize doors, from behind which she could plainly hear a great buzz of conversation.

Then, with a small smile, the Principal opened the door and ushered her in.

Laurel was immediately dazzled by the colour of the Dons' academic robes. Everyone had donned their very best gowns, of course, and she laughed at herself as she realised that her own flame-orange gown was hardly going to be noticed amidst the scarlet, blues, golds, and ermine of the more lavish and senior Fellow's academic garb.

There was the usual sudden lull in conversation as all eyes turned her way. Males eyes opened wide at the vision beside their staid, rather stiff-upper-lip Principal.

Immediately, everyone began to speak again.

Laurel smiled, took a deep breath, and let herself be led into the throng.

Gideon Welles was sitting well out of the mêlée, on a low-slung sofa at the far end of the Senior common room, and so hadn't been able to see the grand entrance. Had he been standing, of course, he would easily have seen, and been seen, over the tops of everyone's heads.

'It looks like our guest of honour has finally arrived, old boy,' the Right Reverend Dr Jimson-Clarke, one of St Bedes' tutors in theology, said quietly.

Since St Bedes had been founded in honour of the Venerable Bede, a noted student of the Benedictine monastery, and author of many works on the saints, St Bedes, naturally enough, had a very strong Theology school.

The Reverend had been happily engaging the Experimental Psychology Fellow in a discussion on the psychology of the Spanish Inquisition, his main field of study. He was just a little miffed to be interrupted.

'It appears so,' Gideon agreed coolly and glanced at his watch. 'I imagine it's still fashionable to arrive late.'

The Reverend, a rather sleepy-eyed, cuddly looking man, smiled knowingly. 'Yes. But then again, if you're bringing with you the gift of so much filthy money, I imagine most of us would wait for your arrival till the Isis froze over.'

There weren't many lucrative chairs going in theology, and Gideon was one of the five shortlisted candidates for the Psychology chair.

'I wonder if the others will think you're grand-standing if you introduce yourself?' the Reverend murmured, with his usual brand of mild mischief and low cunning.

The Reverend's teddy-bear looks hid a very acute brain that held a very real grasp of the world's more iniquitous sins. Too fine a grasp, as most of the undergraduate students had long-since found out.

Now Gideon smiled, far too wily an opponent to take the bait. 'Probably. It's already a little awkward. My being in the shortlist, and with it being St Bedes' turn to host the prize-giving, I mean,' he clarified as his friend raised a questioning eyebrow.

The Reverend, who's given name was Rex, nodded thoughtfully. All the colleges were on a rota system when it came to hosting visiting dignitaries. This year, it was the turn of St Bedes to host the prize-giving for the Van Gilder chair. And, for the first time since its foundation, one of the shortlisted candidates happened to be a member of the host-college.

'But there's no hint of impropriety about it, old boy,' the Reverend assured him jovially. 'The Van Gilder chair is as respectable and as scrupulously honest as it gets.'

Gideon acknowledged this frankly.

Within the University, there was always a lot of politics and jockeying for position. Back-stabbing was an art form in this city.

But the Van Gilder chair was awarded by an independent panel, that was kept scrupulously free of Oxford and back-room manoeuvres.

There were five people shortlisted for the chair – himself, Sir Laurence Fox (who was the oldest of the candidates), an exceptionally able young woman on a Research Fellowship from Nairobi called Dr Julie Ngabe, his old friend and sparing partner, Dr Martha Doyle, and Dr Felicity Ollenbach, a bright rising star who was making a bit of a name for herself as a television personality, since she seemed determined to accept every radio and television appearance that was offered her.

Although, of course, none of these candidates had discussed their chances with the others (that not being the done thing), it seemed to be generally thought that Sir Laurence was the hottest contender.

Of them all, by sheer weight of his years, he had contributed most to the field of Experimental Psychology. Also, since he was mostly lecturing now and on the verge of retirement, he would be in the best position to make use of his time. Financially secure for the next three years, he had it in him to write a work that could keep scholars happy for years to come. Ever since Gideon had known him, he'd always been about to start on a definitive version of a rather intriguing theory on dream interpretation. Always before, he'd had too many other commitments.

'Of course, the Van Gilder people might want much younger blood than old Sir Laurence,' the Reverend mused idly.

'Dr Ngabe, you mean?' Gideon said, missing the fond but slightly exasperated look the Reverend gave him. 'You could be right. She would certainly be a credit to the chair.'

'I meant you, dear boy,' Rex Jimson-Clarke said mildly, and was not surprised to receive a genuinely astonished look in return.

It was an open secret that St Bedes considered Gideon Welles one of the jewels in its academic crown. He'd been their brightest undergraduate for decades and had received a First at twenty-one. He'd stayed with the college to obtain one of the most talked about D.Phil.s in Oxford – and that was saying something! – with a thoroughly revolutionary thesis on…the Reverend frowned. What was it now? Like most scholars, he wasn't much use outside his own particular field of expertise. Well, whatever it was, it was still much talked about, even today, and the amount of pupils applying to read Experimental Psychology at St Bedes was double of any other colleges, simply on the strength of Gideon Welles' Fellowship.

But it was typical of the man not to fully realise his own huge reputation. It was one of the reasons the Reverend liked him so much. Like most true geniuses, he didn't seem to need to be told how wonderfully brilliant he was. Which could be a bit wearing on the nerves, unless you were of a saintly disposition, like himself!

'I say, they're rather queuing up to make a fuss of our American friend, aren't they? She must be a bit of a cracker,' the Reverend mused, craning his neck in a vain bid to catch a glimpse of their American VIP.

Gideon hid a smile at Rex's words, murmured an excuse, and rose from the low-slung sofa with his usual lithe ease.

The moment he stood up, Laurel, of course, saw him. How could she not? One moment she was making polite conversation with a rather fierce Fellow in Astral Psychics or something, the next, a silver head suddenly rose above the throng, like a moon rising.

She knew him instantly. Her heart, for some strange

reason, tripped over itself and she had to stop to take a quick breath.

Luckily, he hadn't seen her.

It hadn't, in fact, even occured to him to look her way, to see what all the fuss was about. The shortlist for the chair had been posted in June but, since then, apart from a forgivable and very human buzz of satisfaction at being mentioned, he hadn't given his actual chances of winning it more than the odd passing thought.

Instead, he made his way to the bar, politely elbowed out an inoffensive little Fellow of St Marks, who'd been talking to the barman about Donne's Metaphysical inaccuracies, and firmly ordered a Cognac.

Socialising was one of his least-favourite pastimes.

A slightly drunk fellow Psychology Don sidled up to him. 'Tell me, how's that graduate student of yours doing, the one who's insisting Freud actually got it all right?' he slurred amiably.

Unfazed, Gideon shrugged. 'Oh, he's still determined to put in a howler of a thesis. But I expect we'll get him to see reason in a few years or so.'

'Well, I suppose I'd better go see a man about a dog,' his companion sighed, and Gideon watched him totter off unsteadily and hoped he'd pass out somewhere inconspicuous.

It was as he was thinking this, that there was a sudden shift of people and Laurel Van Gilder was suddenly revealed, set amidst a frame of chattering Dons.

A lot of Fellows from other colleges had been invited to dine in Hall, and most of them he knew by sight and reputation. So Laurel instantly stood out as a stranger. But in that same split second of seeing her, she looked as familiar to him as his own face.

It was a disorientating moment.

Laurel looked over at him with unchaining timing. She had, in fact, been keeping tabs on him for the last ten minutes, whilst telling herself that she was doing no such thing.

And so their eyes met.

His blue eyes turned to ice. Her own snapped and sharpened.

The maniac on the bike, Gideon thought. What on earth was she doing here?

He walked forward, reluctantly dragging his feet across the common room Aubusson. He didn't really want to do it. He had, in fact, no wish to meet her again and be lashed by that loud and cutting tongue of hers. But, somehow, he was being compelled across that room. Drawn by invisible hands that simply insisted on his being closer to her. Closer. Always closer.

'Ah, and here's our final shortlisted candidate,' Lord St John James said, in his hearty Colonel-about-town manner. 'This is Professor Welles. Gideon, please meet Laurel Van Gilder. She's here to present the chair to its winner.'

It was hard to say, in that instant, which of them was the more surprised.

They were both certainly dismayed.

Laurel, the only one in the room who knew that Professor Welles was in fact the winner, found herself almost wishing that she could arbitrarily award the chair to someone else. That nice Dr Ollenbach, perhaps, a fellow-American who'd been so pleasant to her earlier.

Anyone but him. But of course, she would never be that petty.

Gideon, for his part, found himself wishing that he was somewhere else. Anywhere else!

It had nothing to do with the fact that she was a Van Gilder. Although it would have been nice to have won the chair, it wasn't something that had obsessed him day and night. No, he just didn't want to be around this woman any more than he had to be.

She'd been seriously disturbing his dreams at night as it was. Ever since he'd spent the night at the John Radcliffe Hospital, watching her sleeping face, he'd found that same face haunting his own sleeping hours.

He wouldn't have minded so much. Obviously, such a shock to his system was bound to give his subconscious a kick-start. But these dreams were of such an erotic nature. He'd woken up sweating many a morning, the ghostly-feel of this woman's hand still lingering on his body.

Now he swallowed hard and told himself not to be such a walking stereotype – the Psychology Professor haunted by erotic dreams, for crying out loud! – and reached across to coolly shake her hand.

'Mrs Van Gilder.'

'Miss,' Laurel corrected snappily, and then could have kicked herself. Why had she done that?

Gideon blinked, then half-inclined his head. 'Miss,' he repeated *sotto voce*.

Laurel had to fight, very hard, the urge to kick him right in the shins. Or somewhere even more painful. Damn the man, did he have to look so annoyingly smug? So utterly cool and above it all?

He was dressed in black evening dress and, with his immense lean height and colouring, he looked like an Adonis. His fine-featured face could have been carved from ice though for all the emotion he displayed.

She realised, with a characteristic start of self-awareness, that she was probably only feeling so annoyed because she'd become used to being 'sucked up to'. She'd met the other shortlisted candidates who had all, with the exception of that nice Sir Laurence, been anxious to make a good impression on her.

It had made her feel both uncomfortable – after all, she knew they hadn't won – and, naturally enough, rather flattered. But this iceman was looking at her as if she was something rather disreputable that had wandered in from the streets. Like an alley cat amid a roomful of thoroughbred Persians.

'Professor Welles has recently been published, of course,' the Principal said, seemingly oblivious to the fulminating waves coming off his two companions, and happily burbled on about Gideon's latest academic achievements, whilst Laurel told herself not to be such a jerk. All these Oxford Dons were probably scathing of the rich and non-academic. She was just being overly-sensitive, letting the big oaf get to her.

She smiled sweetly as Sin-Jun (as she would forever think of him), finally came to a halt.

'Well, I'm sure Professor Welles' book will hit the bestseller list in no time. He looks like a male version of Lydia Lovegate to me,' she said naming the current best-selling author of a rather steamy novel that was currently taking American by storm, with a deeply amused twinkle in her dark eyes.

As expected, a look of extreme distaste crossed Gideon's face. Even the Principal looked a bit taken aback.

He'd been listening to the delightful Van Gilder girl all night, and she'd seemed to him a very reasonable and intelligent gal.

'Yes, well, er…' the Principal glanced across at the Dean in a well-rehearsed silent gesture.

'Time for dinner, I think?' the Dean murmured. And, miraculously, those words seemed to reach through the noisy crowded room and turn them all, like a herd of wild deer, toward the direction of Hall.

As he left, Sin-Jun nodded at the Dean, who nodded back. He'd arranged for the Augentine chalice to be set up in the display cabinet whilst they were dining. That way, it could be admired by everyone later on that evening. It was up to the Dean to see that it was locked in place and the security guard dismissed. Naturally, the display cabinet was fitted with a burglar-alarm, but as he escorted his VIP guest to Hall, the College's security system was the last thing on his mind.

Hall, Laurel discovered, was a huge building opposite Webster, one of the three student residences, and consisted of vast kitchens on the bottom floor, and a huge dining room on the top. High Table was set on a dais at the top end of the hall, and was lavishly laid out with all the best college silver.

The lower tables were filled with seated undergraduates, who fell respectfully silent (or rather, less noisy) as the Fellows and their guests took their seats at High Table.

As Laurel sat in her chair in pride of place next to the Principal's throne-like, red velvet chair, she reached for one of the goblets and glanced at it.

She wasn't really up on Heraldry, but the college crest of arms looked to her like a rather splendid and unusual creation in blue, white and black. An upside down 'V' split the shield in half. On the top half were two open books, whilst underneath were three swans. The Latin motto underneath read, 'Murus Aenus Virtus'.

'Virtue is a wall of brass,' a clear but very dry voice said in her ear. Laurel, startled, looked up at the woman seated opposite her. She looked eighty, if she was a day.

The woman smiled at her. 'I'm Daphne Green, the Emeritus Professor of Classics'.

'Oh, I see,' Laurel said, feeling a bit nervous about her own ignorance. 'This silver looks like George III. Is it?'

Before she could answer, another Don further down, who was a noted authority on George III, broke in agreeing with her and gave her a potted history about how the college had been awarded the silver by an ex-pupil who had been, rather unfortunately, hanged by the neck by an ungrateful sovereign after fighting on the wrong side in some war or other.

And so it went on.

As Laurel's head began to swim with the knowledge all these well-meaning Fellows began to pile on top of her head, Gideon watched her with a growing sense of both mirth and despair.

Mirth, because she was so obviously out of her depth around all these academics. And despair because, try as he might, he simply couldn't seem to take his eyes off her.

Damn her, did she have to have such outrageous cheek-bones? And did she have to charm all the older, crustier Dons who still, secretly, preferred their Oxford colleges to be monk-like residences? And did she have to have such an infectious laugh and be quite so outrageously charming?

And why on earth did she have to wear that dress?

He couldn't seem to keep his eyes away from that criss-cross of orange material over her breasts, and he could clearly see her skin glowing in the candlelight.

He drank the excellent Veuve Clicquot from the college's own extensive wine cellar and tried to engage the Fellow on his right, a fine thinker in Modern History, on any subject he cared to mention.

He tried to tune out that distracting American voice, so soft and sultry, that was laughing and teasing old Rex Jimson-Clarke, but it was impossible. Time and time again, his icy blue eyes strayed in her direction. She had the same fascination as a sore tooth.

He was not the only one whose attention was fixed so firmly on Laurel Van Gilder.

A few chairs down and to the right, Dr Ollenbach was anxiously crumbling pieces of bread on to her plate.

I have to get it. If I don't get it, I don't know what I'll do. I simply have to win it. I have to have the money. I must, must, must.

Opposite her, placed between the Dean and the Appeals Secretary, was Martha Doyle, eyeing Laurel Van Gilder with a secretive smile.

Bit of a show-off, that woman. That dress is pure exhibitionism. Wonder if I've got a chance of getting that chair? Probably not. Oh well.

At the far end, Sir Laurence Fox picked at his food.

I'm getting too old for all this rigmarole. I'll be glad to retire. I won't be able to though, if I've won the chair. No, it won't be me. I'll lay odds on Gideon getting it.

And watching the proceedings from the other end of the table, was the calm, lovely face of Dr Julie Ngabe. Her dark eyes gave nothing away, her full and lovely mouth was neither smiling aggressively nor tightly pinched. She looked totally calm.

If they don't give me the Chair, St Joans won't renew my Research Fellowship. Morton hinted as much just yesterday. And if I don't get the chair, I won't be able to afford to stay in Oxford to finish the D.Phil. I'll have to go back to Kenya. And everyone's relying on me back home to do well. I must be in with a chance! Apart from Professor Welles, I'm the only one who's clearly a first-class scholar. It won't be fair if they don't give it to me.

At last, the final course was served.

Lord St John James tapped his wine glass with a spoon and the room fell obediently silent. He rose to his feet to address his troops.

'Ladies and Gentlemen, my esteemed guests,' he nodded at the Fellows from the other colleges, 'and students,' he tossed the room of young men and women an off-hand glance. 'We are gathered tonight to hear Miss Laurel Van Gilder announce the winner of the prestigious Van Gilder chair in Psychology.'

There was a general murmur of polite approval. In his chair, Sir Vivian sighed very loudly and obviously and momentarily put the Principal off his stride.

'Miss Van Gilder, if you please?' he murmured.

Everyone at the High Table leaned forward, even those Dons whose subjects were as far removed from psychology as engineering and modern languages. There was always something electrifying about the awarding of a big prize. The kudos. The money. The fame. It was like being at the Oxford equivalent of the Oscars.

Julie Ngabe's face became even more bland.

Dr Ollenbach suddenly stopped chasing crumbs around her plate.

Martha Doyle smiled wickedly at the sudden air of tension.

Sir Laurence finished off the last of his wine.

Gideon tried not to look at her as Laurel slowly rose to her feet. But failed.

He was used to women being so much smaller than himself, but she looked as if her head would rest in just the right place against his shoulder, if they were to dance.

Damn it, they were never going to dance together. He followed Sir Laurence's example and finished off the last of his wine.

'Thank you, Lord St John James,' Laurel said, her voice slightly husky with all the talking she'd been doing. 'I won't prolong the agony. On behalf of the Van Gilder Foundation, I can tell you that the 2001 to 2004 Chair in Psychology goes to Professor Gideon Welles, of St Bedes College.'

Whereupon, several things happened at once.

The undergraduates, like supporters of a football team that has unexpectedly won the cup, suddenly erupted into spontaneous cheers.

Dr Ngabe's face turned to stone.

Dr Ollenbach quickly and surreptitiously wiped away the tears that were rolling down her face.

And Gideon rose slowly to his feet as Laurel held out her hand, her bold eyes clashing with his.

Slowly, with barely-hidden reluctance, Gideon shook her hand.

Laurel smiled at him grimly through gritted teeth. As they shook hands, she leaned closer and whispered in his ear.

'Considering I've just awarded you a huge amount of money and a prestigious award, you might try to look just a little grateful!'

Gideon smiled. Like a wolf. And raising her hand to his lips, he mockingly kissed her knuckles.

Laurel's knees promptly turned to water.

chapter four

A few minutes later, the Principal began leading the throng back once more to the Senior common room, where the College Butler was busily arranging the port, coffee, and mints.

As they approached the outer door, everyone else tactfully hung back allowing Sin-Jun, Laurel, Gideon and the other shortlisted candidates to enter first.

In the hall, the Dean, hearing someone coming in, turned around looking harassed and already speaking.

'Oh, Principal, just the fellow I needed to see. We have a problem with the alarm,' he began, then broke off instantly as the others came through the door. He flushed painfully at the minor social indiscretion, then coughed into his hand and smiled weakly.

'Welcome back everyone. Everything's ready for you inside.'

He caught Sin-Jun's caustic eye, and Gideon broke into the slightly awkward moment by pushing open the green baize doors and ushering everyone in.

As they filed past, they all glanced at the cabinet where, on the centre shelf and in pride of place, directly in the middle, stood a small, silver cup.

The famous Augentine chalice.

It looked old, but the silver work bore the obvious hand of a master.

When everyone had finally gone through into the Senior common room, the Dean looked at the Principal shame-faced. 'Sorry about that. Didn't realise you had company.'

Sin-Jun waved a hand. 'Never mind that. What's this about the alarm?'

'It was the security guard that had delivered the chalice for Miss Van Gilder who noticed. The alarm must have a short in it somewhere. I promised him I'd stay here and guard it until you came.'

Sin-Jun scowled at the cabinet. He knew exactly how much the fifteenth-century silver chalice was worth. 'You've called the security people?' he demanded. 'Oh yes. They have a twenty-four-hour service,' the Dean assured him. 'But their expert is based in London. It'll take him an hour-and-a-half to get here.'

'Hum. But it's locked?' Sin-Jun asked, reaching out even as he spoke and rattling the cabinet doors which held firm.

'Oh yes,' the Dean assured him hastily.

Conscious of his waiting guests, Sin-Jun nodded. 'Well, I think it's safe enough for an hour or two. No thief's going to chance his arm when there's a roomful of people only a few yards away. But ask Bates in the Lodge to keep a careful eye out for strangers though, just in case.'

Relieved, the Dean nodded and hurried off to do just that. Although a power in his own right within the college's administrative structure, the ex-soldier turned Principal still had a way of making people jump to his orders!

Inside, everyone was drinking coffee and Cognac and spirits were high.

Gideon had an almost constant stream of people queuing up to congratulate him.

'Well, I must say, I'm especially pleased for St Bedes, that our own Fellow has captured the prize, dear lady,'

Sin-Jun said quietly to Laurel. 'Though, of course, I must take time to commiserate with the defeated and walking wounded.'

Laurel gave a noncommittal smile as the older man moved off, but was not really listening. Was that a Stubbs on the far wall? So far, she'd noticed several paintings that belonged in museums, hung with obvious nonchalance, on several of the college walls, both in Hall and in here.

She supposed a college that had been going as long as 'the Venerable' had had more than its share of generous gifts, bequeathed in old member's Last Wills and Testaments. In fact, the whole rarefied atmosphere of the college fascinated her.

More and more, she was coming to see the college not as a collection of Elizabethan buildings, but as a community within a community.

All around her, the guests began to fall on the Port and on one another, several gathering around Gideon with congratulations and cleverly-disguised barbs.

In one corner, Dr Ollenbach restlessly rubbed her thumb over the small diamond pendant she was wearing and eagerly grabbed a glass of champagne from a circulating scout.

Laurel drank in the discreet party atmosphere, networked in a drifting, pleasant way, and finally came to rest in a window seat overlooking the main gardens that were dark and shadowy.

She smiled as the ancient Emeritus Fellow in Classics sidled up to her and took the weight off her varicose veins with a tiny, lady-like sigh of bliss.

'Well, you've certainly tossed a pebble into the peaceful millpond,' the ancient, learned lady said with a distinct twinkle in her water-blue eyes.

Laurel laughed lightly. 'Oh, I only hand out the awards. I leave it to the academic panel to decide who's the most worthy recipient.'

As she spoke, her gaze wandered to the tall silver head as Gideon worked his way around the room and carefully kept as far away from her as possible.

Her lips twisted bitterly, and something of her doubts must have shown on her face, for Daphne Green's twinkling eyes suddenly sharpened.

'And, of course, they've made the right decision,' the old lady said crisply. 'I dare say, as a member of St Bedes you may think I'm biased, but of all the shortlisted candidates, Gideon is by far the most gifted scholar. Dr Ngabe, given a few years, might be his equal but not as it stands now.'

The old lady shrugged delicately.

'He's that good then?' Laurel said quickly.

Too quickly.

Daphne Green was way too wily a bird not to understand what that avid, pink-cheeked interest meant. She'd seen enough girls in her time have the same expression in their eyes.

So. It was like that, was it? Daphne smiled.

At her age, she enjoyed watching the machinations and struggles of the young. It brought back such wonderful memories. Still, she had to keep the faith with her own sex. And Miss Van Gilder needed hard, straightforward, no-nonsense information.

'Oh yes, he's by far one of the three greatest minds at St Bedes,' she said airily but with perfect seriousness. 'The other two being myself, of course, and the Principal. Don't let that widowed, crusty exterior fool you, m'dear,' she said, at Laurel's surprised look. 'Sin-Jun might look like a stereotype of the retired civil-servant of long-standing, with the usual meaningless string of letters behind his name. But he was a lion in his time and once a lion, always a lion. St Bedes has prospered under his captaincy more than under the last three Principals put together. But, of course, it's Gideon you want to know about.'

Laurel opened her mouth to say that she certainly did not, that she couldn't care less if she never found out a single thing about the iceman. But then, she caught the look in the octogenarian's eye and was suddenly too ashamed to deny it.

Daphne smiled and gave a mental nod of approval. Good. It was a rare girl who knew what she wanted.

'Well, in some ways, his is a rather conventional story,' Daphne began, her gaze straying between the tall silver-haired giant and her rapt companion. 'He came to St Bedes as an undergraduate at eighteen, from a large comprehensive school just down the road. Surprisingly, not many locals make it into the University. His parents worked on a farm just outside the city.'

'I don't suppose working on a farm appealed to him one little bit,' Laurel couldn't help but interrupt, somewhat waspishly.

Daphne smiled. Such passion!

My, my, Gideon had better watch himself!

'Well, my dear,' she said mildly, 'I don't suppose truly great scholars ever do. Of course, that was never an issue as far as Gideon was concerned. The poor boy lost both his parents in a car crash when he was in his second year here. Their tied cottage went to someone else which explains, I suppose, how he drifted into letting the college become his home. I'm not sure that's very healthy you know. But there it is.'

Laurel frowned. 'I'm not sure I understand what

you mean.'

Daphne shrugged one bony elbow, wincing at her sciatica. 'Well, my dear, it's like this. The Fellows in this college, like all colleges, fall into two distinct categories. Those that live out with their families, and those that live in. Those that live out have wives and husbands to deal with, kids, mortgages, bills and so forth, and generally have to muck in and live life like most other mortals. But those that live in, well! That's totally different. Their whole lifestyle is much more rarefied. For instance, they have their breakfast brought to them by scouts, they're apt to treat the Senior common room like their own private men's club and are generally prone, over the years, to just sort of fall into the life of a privileged monk. That latter distressing state of affairs is particularly true of St Bedes, unfortunately. The Venerable Bede himself was an Anglo-Saxon historian, devoted to academia. A protégé of the Benedictines, he wrote a lot of hymns, epigrams, and commentaries on the Old and New Testaments. Naturally this college, as a result, has a huge history and theology school and retains, more than any other Oxford College, that monk-like, dry, academic atmosphere that can be so dangerous for single men.'

Laurel gaped at her, trying not to laugh. 'Are you trying to tell me that that…' she looked across the room at Gideon Welles, his classic profile turned and bent to listen to a very annoyingly lovely woman, 'that he…' (damn him, he was so gorgeous!), '…that…'

She was stuttering. Abruptly, she snapped her teeth closed and shook her head.

'I know. Shocking isn't it?' Daphne said, helping her out. After all, if you couldn't speak your mind at eighty when could you? 'He's so tall and good-looking. And cool and aggravating and, I imagine, a quite, quite, spectacular lover. Have you ever noticed his hands?'

Laurel blinked. 'Huh? His hands?'

'No, I suppose the face captivates you too much. And those eyes. But take a look at his hands when you get the opportunity, m'dear. Long, white, sensitive hands. The kind of hands that would know their way about a woman's body, I shouldn't wonder. And all of that going to waste here at good old St Bedes. I've always found it a crying shame.'

Laurel gaped at the old woman, for once in her life, she was stuck for words.

Daphne smilingly accepted a brandy from a scout and told herself off for enjoying herself so much. But, really, it was about time that Gideon was rescued whilst he was still young enough to enjoy it.

'Oh, I have no doubt he's had plenty of women,' Daphne carried on, anxious to correct any misinterpretations the younger woman might have formed. 'Looking like that, after all, he's hardly likely to have gone unnoticed by the female population of a city as big as this, but…' she took a sip of brandy. 'Excellent! But he's always had St Bedes to protect him. Having rooms in college is always such a convenient bolt-hole, don't you think? And the company of his fellow Dons, the glut of intelligent conversation, the pampering, the satisfaction of teaching some of the best minds in the country, all of that gives him the perfect excuse to keep women at a distance. What he needs, of course, is to fall flat-on-his-face in love. That'll teach him!'

Daphne followed Laurel's example and cast a quick look at the object of their discussion. 'Take Martha there, for instance, the woman he's talking to. Martha Doyle. She was on the shortlist for the Van Gilder chair too, mainly for her very good D.Phil. thesis, I should think. Anyway, she's definitely not in Gideon's class as a scholar, of course, but she could talk to him as an equal, she's passably good-looking, and has had the discreet hots for him for years. But does he bite like a good little hooked fish ought to? Not he,' Daphne snorted.

Laurel, who'd been torn between amusement, fascination, and thanking her lucky stars to have found such a generous mine of information as Daphne, began to feel less happy with the way the conversation was turning.

She glanced surreptitiously at the woman still talking to Gideon. She was not young – she had to be in her forties – but she was extremely well-preserved. Her honey-coloured hair was still shoulder-length and wavy. Her figure, though very much more rounded than Laurel's own, was still the kind that men preferred.

'Don't worry m'dear, Martha hasn't got what it takes to winkle our Gideon out of his cosy shell.'

Laurel stiffened. 'I'm not sure that a man like that should be "winkled" out.'

Daphne's eyes positively glittered. 'Don't you think so, m'dear? I rather think it would be fun melting the iceman.'

Laurel turned startled eyes in the older woman's direction. 'So that's how you see him too?'

'Oh yes. But then, that's how he wants the world to see him.'

'You don't think it's an accurate representation of his character?'

Both women turned to look at him then. 'Perhaps,' Daphne said. If the old saying held true, his ears should have been positively roasting at that moment. But he showed no signs of being aware of such intense scrutiny.

Instead, he turned and left the Senior common room,

barely glancing behind him.

'Oh well, I think it's time I climbed the wooden hill to Bedfordshire,' Daphne said, totally baffling her new American friend who wasn't acquainted with the old-fashioned British way of saying she was going to bed. Daphne deposited her empty glass on a coffee table, laid a gnarled hand on Laurel's bare arm, using it to help her struggle back to her feet, and said cheerfully, 'Good hunting m'dear.'

Laurel watched her go, a wide smile on her face. What a game old girl!

She saw the green baize doors open and her heart thumped, but it was Julie Ngabe who entered. Telling herself she was a fool for feeling disappointed, she quickly cut a path to the striking African woman.

'Dr Ngabe, I'm so sorry you were unsuccessful this time,' Laurel said with genuine regret. 'But I'm sure I'll be seeing your name on future shortlists,' Laurel commiserated. 'Tell me about your area of research.'

Julie Ngabe, showing no signs of unease, gave a long but surprisingly easy-to-follow résumé of her work. Then, glancing over Laurel's shoulder, she murmured something polite and drifted away.

'I see my colleague is through monopolising you,' a dry, cold voice spoke from the rarefied air several inches above her head.

Laurel turned, annoyed at having to look so far up. She wasn't used to it and wasn't sure she liked it. 'Dr Ngabe has been wonderful,' she said firmly. And her eyes glittered, like an eagle spotting a rabbit.

Gideon's blue eyes narrowed.

Laurel's wide smile widened even further.

Suddenly, remembering Daphne's words, she dropped her eyes to his hands. Her breath caught. Daphne had been right, he did have fantastic looking hands.

Ten minutes later, a figure slipped quietly out of the Senior common room.

Nobody in the throng noticed the departure.

Barely fifteen minutes later, the absentee was back again and chatting to Rex Jimson-Clarke.

In one corner, Martha Doyle began to get rather drunk.

It was, in many ways, a typical Oxford college party.

chapter five

'I expect you're waiting for me to thank you?' Gideon had once more bit the bullet and decided to corner Laurel Van Gilder for a second time.

After the Emeritus Fellow and Dr Ngabe had finished talking to her and left, he'd felt it was high time to get things sorted out once and for all. He'd marched across, fully prepared to act like a reasonable human being only to be treated to the American wench's double-talk.

And why had she kept staring at his hands?

Gideon had retreated almost immediately after that little episode, all the reconciling and civilised things he'd intended to say left humiliatingly unsaid. Instead, he'd tried to enjoy the party.

Without success.

It was not like him to be slightly confused. Always before, he'd been in complete charge of both himself and the situation.

People had a habit of coming to him when they were in trouble sensing, perhaps, that he was the one person they could rely on to be both unbiased, fair, and experienced enough to help. In his time, he'd sorted out suicidal undergraduates, fellow Dons' marriage crises, and numerous rows.

He'd always been able to rely on himself to meet any situation with a level head, practical compassion, and gentle understanding.

Laurel Van Gilder, on the other hand, had him see-sawing up and down like a demented yo-yo. And it had to stop!

The party was now beginning to wind down. As the hour of midnight approached, Fellows reluctantly began to remember the tutorials they had scheduled for tomorrow. Guests from other colleges contemplated the state of their own heads come the morning. The Port, it had to be said, had been liberally flowing.

Reluctantly, slowly, people were beginning to drift away. The volume of noise slowly decreased.

Gideon, as the 'star attraction' was more than ready to call it a night also. The unexpected windfall of winning the prestigious Van Gilder chair was, of course, a very pleasant surprise, but it was not what held his attention.

That American woman seemed to be haunting him.

Eventually, he'd been forced to approach her one last time in order to offer at least some sort of olive branch. They simply couldn't go on like this.

So why, oh why, he thought with a mixture of frustration and surprise, had his first words been so antagonistic?

Laurel spun around, suddenly hearing that oh-so-familiar voice, with its usual mocking tones. The overhead light caught the silver and amber beads in her hair as she did so, causing a stray spark of light to shine in his eyes.

Gideon winced at the sudden glimmer of light, then tensed as he watched that familiar wide-mouthed smile suddenly light her face.

He knew he was in for it, even before she spoke.

'Professor Welles. Did you say something?' she asked sweetly.

'I said,' Gideon gritted, 'that I imagine you're waiting for me to thank you?' he repeated, knowing full well that she'd heard him the first time and was only making him repeat his mistake for the sheer devilry of it.

Laurel caught the angst in his voice, carefully concealed though it was, and felt her smile widen.

Really, this man was an awful lot of fun.

It was a bit like poking a sleeping tiger with a stick. Just the right amount of pressure and he twitched in his sleep, leaving you to clap your hands in glee and try again. Too much and grrrrr!

'Why, Professor Welles, the thought never even crossed my mind.' She smiled even more sweetly, revealing a gleaming row of snow-white teeth.

Gideon's own teeth clenched. 'Meaning that you've already made up your mind that I'm...what? Too ungrateful? Too arrogant? Too blasé?'

Laurel laughed openly. 'Now why should I think any of those things, Professor? It isn't as though you've given me any reason to think so. Is it?'

Gideon found himself taking an impulsive step towards her and halted abruptly.

Behind him, he could hear Martha Doyle cheerfully calling goodbye to Rex Jimson-Clarke. To his right, the Principal's deep tones were making goodbye noises to Julie Ngabe.

Now was definitely not the time to raise his voice or lose his temper. Not that he would anyway. This woman didn't have what it took to get to him.

Yeah. Right.

He gave her his own sweet smile right back. And if he'd allowed his eyes to drop to the swell of her breasts, he'd have seen her nipples suddenly strain and burgeon against the flame-coloured silk.

As it was, Laurel managed to keep her purely instinctive and devastatingly sexual reaction to that spine-tingling smile from showing on her face, at least.

But her legs went treacherously weak.

'As you say,' Gideon said smoothly, 'I've always been taught to act like the perfect gentleman. Even if kamikaze females will throw their bikes at my car. Incidentally, you'll be receiving a bill for damage to my Morgan's paintwork.'

The smile he now gave her was absolutely dazzling. 'Goodnight, Miss Van Gilder. I do hope the rest of your stay in England will be less dramatic.'

And with that very excellent exit line, he turned on his heel and headed back into the diminishing throng of the party…feeling alternately elated and thoroughly ashamed of himself.

He'd thought he'd got over playing such childish games years ago.

Laurel, caught on the hop, had no choice but to watch him go, her mouth hanging open, a smile fighting its way to her face.

Perfect gentleman?

And a bill for his car repairs? Of all the damned cheek. Of all the insufferable behaviour.

The party gradually fizzled out. People began to make their way to St Bedes' two small car parks, one opposite the college clock, the other facing the college War Memorial, both of which were at opposite ends of Wallace Quad.

It was dark and dimly lit outside. Some of the party-goers who lived nearby had been able to drink their fill and now headed towards the main gates to walk home. Other's cadged lifts.

Those present who lived-in had the easiest route home of all and merely crossed the gardens to Wolsey or Walton, or crossed Wallace Quad to Webster, the college's three main residences, where students and Dons lived alike in splendid and ancient rooms.

The Fellows of St Bedes had rooms scattered throughout the college's residences, which were all named after noted personages. So it was that everyone wandered off everywhere, nobody taking particular notice of who went where, when, and in what order. Why should they?

And so it was that later, no one was able to accurately give the police a clear-cut description of that evening's events.

Only one thing would become crystal clear.

The Augentine chalice had been stolen!

Laurel Van Gilder stepped briskly from the Senior common room at St Bedes and into the Hall.

There she walked past the cabinet, glancing at it in order to look at the chalice. Although, technically, it belonged to her, in truth she couldn't remember ever having seen it before. Although the Van Gilder Art Collection was now her inheritance, it had always been the baby of one of her aunts, who held a degree in Fine Art from the Sorbonne.

But as she glanced at the cabinet, she saw that it was covered by a big heavy black coat. Obviously the coat racks had been full, and someone had simply tossed his coat across it.

She shrugged, moving on through the hall and out into the night.

She'd managed to give Sin-Jun the slip, knowing that he'd insist on escorting her to the main gates and helping her into her taxi. Such old-world gallantry was very pleasant, of course, but the truth was she wasn't ready to go just yet.

It was dark outside and she stood for a few seconds in the car park, looking around.

Most of the cars were facing the postern gate, not the quad and, even as she watched, a car engine rumbled and headlights lit up the wall that ran the length of the tiny alleyway.

The car pulled out of the college grounds and left her peering once more into the dark.

With a mental map of the college grounds in her head, she followed the line of wall that led off to her left and came to the Becket Arch, a medieval structure that led her into the main gardens.

In the moonlight, she could just make out the silver reflection of the moon on the still waters of the pond.

Setting off on the gravel paths that led between the rose bushes, she made her way towards the bottom left hand side of the college and the residence called Wolsey. She'd rather cleverly winkled out of a tipsy Modern History Don, the name and number of Gideon Welles' rooms.

After she'd turned her back for a moment and found him gone – the rotten sneak – she'd become more and more determined to have it out with him once and for all.

The fact that now, with the Van Gilder chair safely delivered to its winner, she had no further excuse to see Gideon Welles had nothing to do with it.

She simply objected, on principle, to a man getting the last word.

As she passed the pond, she could see a big dark shape move in the depths and she wondered how many of the big carp the pond housed.

For some reason, she shivered.

It was not just the clammy coldness of the early November night either. Shadows seemed to writhe in the creeper that covered the walls of the ancient library, away to her right.

She half-expected an owl to hoot, as it did in all the best horror movies.

She was glad to reach the main door to Wolsey and then, a moment later, could have kicked herself for being so stupid. The door was locked, of course. It was well after midnight.

Damn, she fumed silently. Was the whole world against her?

It seemed not however. For just as she was turning away, she heard a tuneless whistle and the ever-present sound of a bicycle. It was being wheeled up the concrete path skirting the residence and a moment later, an undergraduate appeared. He propped the bicycle in one of the many bicycle racks littered around the college, bent down to chain it firmly, and then walked towards her, his head down as he rifled his pockets for his keys.

Laurel took a step back.

The young man's head reared up as he sensed the movement, and she saw him grin widely as he took in her slender form.

'I'm just waiting for, er, someone to come down,' Laurel lied glibly.

The undergraduate laughed benevolently. 'Hang on a tick, I can save him the trouble.'

He opened the door, standing ostentatiously to one side to allow Laurel through.

A single lamp burned in a large, cold, vestibule.

To her relief, the student (who obviously had rooms on the top floor) immediately bolted for the wide, wooden staircase and noisily took the steps two at a time.

Laurel knew that Gideon had rooms on the ground floor, overlooking the gardens, and she began to peer in the dim light at the room numbers.

She found his room unexpectedly quickly, and then

had to wait outside his door, shuffling from one foot to the other, working up the nerve now that she was actually here to knock on the wooden door.

She glanced around curiously. The diamond-shaped panes of glass glinted in the moonlight. There was the faint smell of lavender furniture polish in the air. Everything was as quiet as a grave.

And, again, Laurel found herself shivering. Crossly, she wondered why she was feeling so fey. Normally she was a robust realist but tonight, for some strange reason, she was as nervous as a skittish deer.

Something, somewhere, was not right.

She shook her head angrily. Damn it, this would not do. She reached forward and tapped on the door. Not quite as loudly as she would have liked, but loudly enough to be unmistakable.

A moment later, the solid and heavy wooden door swung open. He was so tall, his head almost touched the top of the door lintel.

'Yes? Miss Van Gilder?'

The first syllable was soft. The rest of his sentence was anything but.

'Professor Welles. I wanted to have a word with you,' she began firmly.

'At this hour of the night? I assumed the evening had all but ended?'

Laurel gritted her teeth. 'It has. There's just Sin-Jun and a few others still to leave.'

One of his silken, silver eyebrows rose.

Laurel took another deep breath. 'Are you going to invite me in? Or are you going to make me stand out here in the cold all night?' she asked tersely.

Gideon felt a wave of heat rise and fall in his face and, before he could stop himself, he was standing back, silently gesturing for her to enter.

'Please. Come in.'

Laurel walked inside and stood looking around.

There was a real fire, in a real grate, blazing away merrily against one wall. The other walls were covered with shelves of books. Two doors led off from the room, no doubt one to his bedroom, the other to either a bathroom or kitchenette. Two old leather armchairs, with shinny patches on both arms, stood facing the fire. A round oak table, polished until it gleamed, was completely bare except for a vase of fresh, bronze chrysanthemums. Their distinctive scent tantalised the air that played host to other similarly evocative scents.

Old books.

Pipe tobacco.

Perfume.

Laurel felt herself tense, then abruptly realised that, of course, he held tutorials in this room and, just as it should be, Oxford had as many female students as it had male.

'Is there something specific you wanted?' Gideon prompted impatiently.

Laurel dragged her fascinated gaze away from the dusty, dark emerald-green velvet curtains and matching sofa covers and turned once more to the man himself.

There was only one lamp burning, and it cast a golden glow over the left side of his face and hair.

He had changed out of his evening suit and was now wearing a long maroon dressing gown, belted at his waist, that fell almost to his ankles.

His feet, she noticed, were bare. It gave him an oddly out-of-place aura of vulnerability.

She swallowed and hastily looked away.

On any man she knew, the dressing gown would have

looked faintly ridiculous. On this man, it looked devastating. His lean waist, the towering height of his figure, and the silver-gold hair contrasting against the deep, ripe colour.

'Miss Van Gilder?' he said sharply.

He didn't like that look in her eyes one bit. It was like being eaten alive.

He could feel his blood begin to simmer. Simultaneously, he became aware of the hardness of his nipples, rubbing against the silk lapels of his dressing gown.

He was having trouble breathing, suddenly, and…

Yes. He was growing hard.

He turned abruptly, walking towards one of the chairs and reached for a book from one of the shelves. Any book.

He turned, the lower part of his body thankfully concealed behind the chair. He glanced down disinterestedly at the book in his hand.

It was one of his own, on animal behaviour!

For some reason, he had to fight the sudden urge to laugh.

He wasn't sure why he was feeling so challenged. Normally women didn't have this effect on him. Over the years, he'd had to deal (patiently and sensitively) with women undergraduates who'd had a crush on him and, more happily, with any number of lovers.

But no other woman had ever made him feel this out of control. And he didn't like it. Not one little bit.

A relationship was approached with honesty, simplicity, and clear-cut goals. Using this method, he'd always parted on the best of terms with his lovers and had never 'broken' a single heart.

This wild, roller-coaster ride was strictly for the birds. And it was disconcerting to find himself suddenly booked on a seat in the front carriage!

He forced himself to glance across at Laurel, daring his heartbeat to leap.

It dared.

'You had something urgent to say, Miss Van Gilder?' he asked flatly and determinedly business-like.

Laurel growled. 'Damn it, do you have to sound so supercilious?'

Gideon blinked, then fought the smile that tugged at his lips. So, the ultra-confident, mega-sophisticated Van Gilder heiress was feeling just a tad unsure of herself too, was she? Good. It would probably do her the world of good.

He sighed heavily. 'I seem to have the rather unfortunate knack of rubbing you up the wrong way, Miss Van…'

'Call me Miss Van Gilder one more time and I'll throttle you,' Laurel said softly. 'My name is Laurel.'

Gideon drew his breath in sharply. 'Very well. Laurel.'

He had to grit the word out. Damn her, why couldn't she just go!

Here he was, trying to the keep the formalities between them, and here she was, just as busily breaking them down.

He glanced at his watch – which wasn't there since he'd already taken it off – and was forced to lower his bare wrist again.

Laurel noticed the gesture and the bare skin, and had to laugh. He looked so disgusted with himself.

Gideon felt himself colouring and gritted his teeth. Never before had he felt so gauche. 'Exactly what can I…' he swallowed hard as Laurel quickly removed her coat, revealing large expanses of bare skin. In a crowded room, it hadn't been too bad but here, alone in his sanctuary, Gideon was hideously aware of his own near-nakedness under the dressing gown.

'... do for you, Miss...' he continued gruffly, but at this her head shot up warningly. '...Laurel,' he finally managed to finish his sentence.

Laurel smiled. 'I wanted to talk to you. About the chair.'

Gideon slowly lifted one eyebrow. 'Oh? Funny. I could have sworn you came here about something else.' As rattled as he was, he wasn't about to let her get away with so much as an inch.

'Well, I didn't,' she snapped, once more lying through her eye teeth. 'I'm just anxious that there should be no...ill feeling about it.'

Laurel looked at the disbelief in his icy blue eyes and was instantly prepared to do battle. Even if she couldn't confess to be fighting on the side of the angels, this time. She was being bloody-minded just for the sake of it, and she knew it.

But how could she explain to this iceman that this was her first assignment as head of the family, and that it was important to her that all should run smoothly?

There was no way in the world that a man as sure of himself as he was, could understand her own lack of self-assurance.

What was it about this man? He could set her off ticking like a time-bomb with just one haughty look and, the next instant, a simple gesture or near-smile would defuse her.

'I can assure you, there's no ill-feeling on my part,' he said glibly and headed firmly towards the door. 'So, I'll say good...'

'Not so fast!' Laurel snapped, her voice cutting across the gentility of the room like a crude bowie knife. Say what you like, Laurel Van Gilder was simply not used to men who scorned her company.

Gideon jerked to a halt. As he did so, his dressing gown swung open slightly just at the knee, revealing a long length of lightly-muscled calf.

Laurel swallowed and dragged her eyes back to his face.

And wished she hadn't. Those eyes were like lasers.

She saw his hands fall to his belt and tighten it.

That defensive gesture, for some reason, seemed to cause an eruption deep inside her. 'For pity's sake,' she snarled. 'What do you think I'm going to do? Throw you to the floor and ravage you?'

Gideon's nostrils flared. 'I should like to see you try, Miss Van Gilder.'

'Would you?' Laurel said. 'Would you?' And found herself moving.

Gideon took a startled step back, bumping painfully against a shelf full of books.

Laurel took a firm grip on his dressing gown, and felt the silk lapels running coldly against her fingers. Her hands curled around them, her knuckles brushing against the warmth of the skin on his chest.

'What on earth are you doing?' Gideon gasped. Because, once again, he could feel that blaze of heat, that sudden surge of urgent, devastating want.

She was suddenly so close. So overwhelming close.

'I thought you'd just invited me to ravish you?' Laurel said shakily, as she wondered exactly what she was doing here. Holding this man by the lapels, pressing up against him, so mad she could spit, so hungry for the touch of him she could purr.

Gideon opened his mouth, but couldn't think of a single thing to say.

He shut it again, and the clicking of his strong white

teeth sounded unusually loud in the fraught silence of the room.

Laurel's eyes darkened to midnight.

Gideon felt a sudden shudder of pure delight race up his spine, making him shiver.

'Oh hell,' Laurel said. And kissed him.

She had to stand on tip-toe to do it, and he did absolutely nothing to help her! But it was the best kiss she could ever remember.

His lips, so slack with surprise in that first instant suddenly responded.

He did it so reluctantly, grudgingly, but also so compulsively, that she felt a shimmer of pure sexual power race through her.

Then she was leaning harder against him and felt something pressing against her stomach.

He was hard! As hard as iron. The sneaky little so-and-so, thinking he could hide it from her!

She pressed herself hard into him, grinding against him, feeling him jump and shimmer. Her breasts flattened against his ribs, and her hands reached up to cup the side of his face, then went down to rest against his chest.

The iceman didn't feel so cold tonight!

Under her fingers, she could feel his heart thundering, like a trapped wild animal.

His lips clung to hers, tasting masculine-sweet.

And, suddenly, something else happened. She wasn't the aggressor any more. She wasn't angry. Wasn't intent on winning their game of one-up-manship. It was as if her own nature had tricked her. Had manoeuvred her into this man's embrace. She felt his arms move around her, holding her and, although it had never happened before, the capture of her body felt dizzily familiar. It was as if they'd done this before. Somewhere. Sometime.

But she knew they hadn't.

Gideon felt his palms burning, as they pressed against the bare skin of her back. Could feel his head begin to pound with the same urgent rhythm that was pounding throughout his body. She seemed to be melting into him.

Her taste was in his mouth. Her scent was in his nose. The sound of her soft breathing was filling his ears. Even the tiny moan she was making, turned into a vibration that seemed to be drilling through his very blood and bone and sinew.

With a wordless, inarticulate, sharp cry of pure panic, he suddenly pushed her away.

Laurel staggered back, brutally yanked back to reality. She stood for several seconds, her ebony eyes blank, aware only of a sense of loss. She'd been somewhere where she'd always wanted to be and now she was somewhere else.

In a room, with a fire and books and a man looking at her with eyes of ice. A man who'd just pushed her out of Paradise.

'Damn you,' Laurel said softly. 'What did you have to go and do a thing like that for?'

Gideon's eyes widened. 'Me?' he yelped, his voice several octaves higher than normal.

He wanted to rub the back of his hand across his mouth, eradicate the taste of her lips, the pressure of her mouth on his. But, somehow, he couldn't command his arm to move.

He leaned back against the books, his big body trembling.

Laurel shook her head dazedly. She felt confused and, worse, scared.

Something had just changed her life for ever and she

wasn't sure she liked it. Wasn't sure she wanted even to believe it.

'I have to go,' she said abruptly and reached for her coat.

Gideon watched her leave, too stunned to move, and within moments she'd walked to the door, opened it, and was gone.

Instantly the room seemed flat. Colder. Emptier. Suddenly, it seemed unfamiliar. This place, where he'd lived for over ten years!

He stared at the door, a baffled, bewildered look on his face.

Outside, Laurel trekked straight across the grass, oblivious of the damage her spiky high-heeled shoes must be doing to the immaculate, centuries-old lawn.

She just couldn't believe she'd actually made such a stupid fool of herself. Throwing herself at him. What must he have thought?

She marched through Becket Arch and into the car park. As she passed Webster, the door opened and a late guest left the party.

She wasn't sure what made her do it. She hadn't even been thinking about the chalice. But, perhaps, her subconscious had been prodding her in this direction ever since she'd first noticed the coat obscuring the cabinet.

Whatever it was, Laurel decided, she wanted to study the ancient piece of silver. It was, after all, part and parcel of the Van Gilder chair in Psychology and if, in some future date, a journalist asked her about it and she couldn't even describe it properly, it would be embarrassing to say the least. Also (she could almost hear her father's voice so strongly did the words come into her head), it would be terrible not to thoroughly acquaint herself with the Van Gilder Art Collection.

Her aunt was very territorial about it but even she would see that, as the new Van Gilder ambassador, it was the sort of thing that Laurel needed to know about.

Making a mental note to study the collection when she got back to the States, she walked once more towards Webster.

The hall was deserted when she stepped inside, and she was rather annoyed to see the big black coat was still draped over the cabinet.

Seeing that there were now plenty of coat-hooks available on the side of the wall, she walked forward and pulled the coat off intending to hang it up properly.

But instead, she stood stock still staring in front of her, the coat clasped, forgotten, to her breast.

The cabinet still housed the Rowing Blues and other assorted trophies.

But it also sported something else.

A round hole in the glass.

And an empty space where, just hours before, the Augentine chalice had stood.

chapter six

Laurel stared at the cabinet in blank dismay for quite a while, her mind working feverishly.

Inside, she felt cold and numb. This was the very last thing she needed. It was, in fact, the one thing in the world it was her job to prevent.

Scandal.

Mud sticking to the Van Gilder name.

So what if it wasn't her fault that the Augentine chalice was gone. Missing.

Stolen.

She forced herself to say the word in her head. Stolen. It was stolen.

It would get into the papers. It was inevitable. Sin-Jun would call in the police. There would be publicity, bad publicity, and it wouldn't matter a whit to her mother, uncles, aunts and cousins, that it had been none of her doing.

It was her job now to make sure this sort of thing didn't happen!

Her very first mission and it was a disaster.

Laurel became slowly aware that she was taking in great big gulps of air. She was close to panicking and she knew it. She had to pull herself together.

Do something.

The Senior common room lay only a few feet away but, surprisingly, she didn't even think of going in there. There were probably still a few late die-hards inside, and Sin-Jun as well who, as host, was bound to stay until the last reveller had left.

But instead of seeking solace and help there, Laurel found herself turning away. No, running away – belting for all she was worth back to Wolsey.

It was a wonder, in her high heels, that she didn't fall and break her neck but a few moments later, she was hammering on the main door to the residence which was once again locked.

Gideon vaguely heard the pounding through the heavy doors and, still restless and angry after his recent tussle with Laurel Van Gilder, growled angrily and jerked open his door, striding across the dark and cold hall towards the main door.

He'd put on pyjamas under his dressing gown, but his feet were still bare. He yanked open the door, half-expecting to encounter a drunken undergraduate, and getting ready to read the riot act.

Instead, nearly six feet of beautiful, distraught female launched herself into his arms.

'Stolen!' Laurel said, quite distinctly, but with an obvious edge of hysteria in her voice.

Gideon, who had her firmly by the upper arms, pushed her a little away, the better to get a look at her, and blinked.

'What? What's been stolen,' he demanded crisply.

'The chalice,' Laurel's teeth had started to chatter.

For an instant, Gideon wanted to laugh, to shake her by the arms and tell her that one drama was more than enough for one night.

But in the pale dingy light of the hall, he could see her sickly pallor, the eyes large and dilated in shock, and felt a cold shiver run down his spine.

'What do you mean?' he asked calmly, carefully enunciating each syllable.

'Senior common room cabinet. Hole in the glass. Gone.'

Laurel found herself speaking in harsh guttural syllables, suddenly unable to string a coherent sentence together.

Gideon stared at her for a few seconds, then gently pushed her towards the interior of the building. 'Go into my rooms. Pour yourself a brandy – it's in the cupboard near the window. Sit down and wrap yourself in something warm. And stay there.'

He was already stepping outside, rather belatedly realising that he hadn't any slippers or a torch. But instead of going back inside for them like any other sensible person, he found himself running across the lawns, glad of the carpeting grass.

As he ran, his agile brain was already leaping ahead, seeking direction. He remembered coming back from dinner and the Dean saying something about the alarm being faulty.

And if he'd heard it, so had the others with him. Martha, Dr Ngabe, Dr Ollenbach, Sir Laurence. His thoughts stopped abruptly as he passed through Becket Arch and he yelped, his running feet suddenly and painfully hitting gravel. He hopped to an agonised stop, cursing himself, but all the time wondering why he was taking it for granted that the chalice had really been stolen.

It was so fantastic.

Things like that didn't happen in Oxford. And certainly not in a college as old and as respectable as St Bedes.

The Van Gilder woman was obviously nearly hysterical.

But not stupid.

It was as if he'd been expecting something bad to

happen all night long. Which was absurd.

As he tip-toed in and carefully approached the college clock, it began chiming the half-hour.

He stepped into the hall outside the Senior common room and saw at once the scene, just as she'd described it.

Incredible.

But it had happened. He himself had seen the chalice in there on their return from dinner. When he'd left, hadn't something big and dark been covering the cabinet? He looked down and saw a big black coat he vaguely recognised as belonging to the College Butler, lying on the floor. He didn't know then that it was Laurel who'd dropped it there.

He glanced inside just long enough to make sure that the chalice was indeed gone. But, unlike Laurel, however, he didn't forget the proximity of the Senior common room and knew his first priority was to alert the Principal.

Although it was half-past midnight, he didn't doubt that there were still a few stragglers around finishing off the Napoleon brandy.

He moved to the green baize doors, pushed them a little open, and peered inside. Mindful of his state of undress and instinctively going into 'damage limitation' mode, he only half-looked in, careful to hide the bulk of his body behind the doors.

Several Dons were grouped around the fireplace, pleasantly dopey and tipsy. The College Butler, sure enough, was still circulating with drinks.

Sir Roland St John James himself was just in the process of dismissing the Butler for the night, a sure hint to the others that it was time to call it a day.

He caught the slight movement of the door, turned, and

raised an eyebrow in shocked disbelief at the sight of the Experimental Psychology Fellow stood there in his pyjamas. Then he noticed the man's paleness and narrowed his eyes at the beckoning finger Gideon crooked his way.

Sin-Jun took a quick look around, satisfied himself that nobody else had caught sight of Gideon Welles, and moved to the door, stepping through in one fluid moment and ushering the Dons back out into the hall. He closed the door quickly behind him.

'My dear chap,' he began. Even if the man had been celebrating his well-deserved victory, it didn't give him the right to make a scene.

'The Augentine chalice has been stolen,' Gideon said flatly.

For one second, Sin-Jun said, did, and thought nothing. Then his training took over. As an ex-soldier, Sin-Jun had had his fair share of dealing with crises.

He strode to the cabinet, stared at it, noted the coat on the floor, frowned, and then glanced at Gideon.

'Tell me what happened,' Sin-Jun said, his voice grim.

Briefly, Gideon related Laurel Van Gilder's abrupt intrusion into Wolsey and her tale of the missing chalice. His own part in checking out her claim was even more briefly explained.

By the time he'd finished, Sin-Jun was already thinking ahead. He said simply, 'I've got to call old Fishers.'

Old Fishers was Chief Constable Stanley Fisher, an old St Marks man, and one of Sin-Jun's many cronies. In confirmation of this, the Principal muttered grimly, 'He'll be able to keep a lid on all this.'

It was typical of the man that, in any crisis, his duty came first. Whether it be to Queen, country, or St Bedes.

Gideon hoped that the Chief Constable would indeed be able to keep it quiet, but surely that depended on getting the chalice back quickly.

And on Laurel agreeing to be reasonable.

His lips twisted wryly as he pondered on the chance of that!

Then, ever-practical, he nodded towards the door behind them.

'What about the others? In the Senior common room.'

Sin-Jun stooped and picked up the coat and draped it across the cabinet. And wondered how many others had innocently left the party, passing the cabinet, unaware of the theft within.

Gideon was thinking the same thing. Once again, he felt himself shudder. It was incredible that a thief should have boldly come in and stolen it when they'd all been only a few yards away. He paused. But how would a thief even know it was there? It was a secret that Gideon had won the chair, and it would be until tomorrow, at the very earliest, when the papers announced it. So how did a burglar know?

It had to be one of them!

No. Gideon shook his head. It was a stupid, idiotic thought. Who at the party tonight would possible want to steal the chalice? They were, one and all, men and women of reputation. Standards.

Suddenly, Sin-Jun stiffened. 'Are the main gates still open?' he asked briskly.

'I think so. They usually are whenever we have a late night.'

'And the posterns?'

Gideon nodded at the postern gates leading into the car park. 'Those are – they have to be. But I think all the others have been locked, as usual, at ten o'clock.'

The Principal nodded. 'So anyone could have got in off the streets and done this.'

'Not through the main gates,' Gideon demurred. 'Jenkins would have seen them.'

The Principal didn't doubt it. St Bedes had a redoubtable Head Porter in Jenkins. Many a time, a male student had tried to sneak past Jenkins, in the pursuit of amour, and felt his collar pinched instead. Mind you, a bottle of Scotch might persuade him to pretend it had never happened.

Jenkins hadn't had to buy his own booze in years.

Gideon grimaced but understood what the Principal was thinking. Oxford, like any big city, had its fair share of drug addicts. Wretched individuals who mugged and robbed in order to feed their habit.

But still.

Gideon stirred restlessly. 'If it was someone from outside,' he said quietly.

Sin-Jun turned and looked at the younger man openly.

'I think you should keep that thought to yourself for the moment, hum, Gideon old boy?' he said. 'After all, it would be to everyone's advantage if we, er, instigated some discreet enquiries ourselves and got the chalice back before any real harm is done. Yes? Come to that, I could always hold off calling Fishers for a day or two.'

Gideon looked at the old man with respect. So that's what he was thinking, was it?

'But what if we don't get the chalice back quickly?' he asked.

Sin-Jun ran a hand thoughtfully across his chin. 'We'll cross that bridge when we come to it,' he said grimly. No doubt the police would not be at all impressed if they were forced to call them in when there'd already been a delay of a few days.

Still, a man had to take chances.

'In the meantime,' he mused, straightening his shoulders, 'we've got to come up with a good cover story to explain the absence of the chalice. Being cleaned? Something along those lines?' he suggested.

Gideon sighed. He still wasn't convinced but he was more than willing to let his Principal have the final say. 'All right.'

'You'll need to speak to Miss Van Gilder. See if you can't persuade her to give us some time before calling in the police herself,' the Principal said, missing the appalled look Gideon gave him.

Then Sin-Jun, taking in the Experimental Psychology Don's bare feet and thin clothing, sighed wearily. 'Go back to your rooms and have a glass of brandy, old boy. You need it.'

'But...'

'Didn't you say that Miss Van Gilder is waiting for you back there? I dare say it's been a bit of a shock to her. And you're by far the best man to see to her.'

Gideon couldn't help but grin wryly at that statement, and was glad the moon had once again headed for cover, leaving them in darkness.

He was the last person to offer Laurel Van Gilder psychiatric advice, but he could hardly say so.

Come to that, he was also probably the last man in the world she would agree to help out but that, again, was something he could hardly explain here and now.

Besides, he wondered if having the police called in right away might not be the best course, after all.

'I'll do my best,' he said wearily, but he fully expected to be talking to the police before the night was out. He doubted Laurel Van Gilder had ever had anything but her own way her whole life through.

And why should she agree to help St Bedes out of their current crisis?

Gideon left, wincing at his now raw feet.

Lord St John James watched him go, his eyes thoughtful and not unsympathetic. Gideon didn't know it yet, but Sin-Jun fully expected Gideon to be the one to track down their thief. He was, the Principal thought, by far the obvious choice. His psychological training alone would surely help him ferret out the lies, neurosis, or outright greed of the culprit responsible.

Laurel Van Gilder was obviously head-over-heels about the man, so he was sure to get her on his side too, Sin-Jun added in mental afterthought.

And, of course, he realised smugly, it wouldn't take Gideon long to realise that he himself was also very much on the suspect list and would need, if nothing else, to clear his own name and reputation.

Sin-Jun, like most old soldiers, could be quite ruthless when he wanted to be.

Dr Julie Ngabe paced about in her little flat just off Canterbury Road, overlooking the Nissan Institute of Japanese Studies.

She was still fully dressed and her robes swung angrily around her feet as she paced up and down, up and down, staring at the telephone.

She had promised to call her mother, all those thousands of miles away, as soon as she'd heard the results of the prize-giving.

But now she just didn't have the heart. Didn't want to hear the disappointment in her mother's voice. Didn't want to have to admit to failure.

Her parents had worked hard, no slaved, to educate their daughter to the degree that had allowed her to gain a two-year Research Fellowship to an Oxford college.

Other parents would have insisted their sons have the education, but they had been wise and strong-minded enough to realise that Julie's brothers didn't have one-tenth of Julie's brains.

She had needed to be awarded the Van Gilder chair in order to stay on and get her D.Phil.

Now her money had run out, her college would not renew the Fellowship, and she'd have no choice but to return to Kenya...and her disappointed family.

Of course, Gideon Welles had always been the main opposition. And he was a very fine scholar. Even so, he didn't actually need the chair. He had tenure for life at St Bedes. A secure future. An academically recognised persona.

It was not fair!

Julie carried on pacing. Agitated. Angry. And afraid. Deathly afraid.

Dr Felicity Ollenbach was in the shower. She was not so much standing, as lolling under the hot, needle-sharp spray, one hand steadying herself against the slippery tiled wall.

She was crying, although the spray hid the fact which was just as well because, suddenly, the curtain was thrust open and a youngish, sleek, good-looking man stood there, glowering at her.

'But I thought you said you had it in the bag?'

The voice was petulant, as was the set of the handsome man's lips. 'That there would be no problem?'

Clive Westlake was an Englishman, several years younger than Felicity, and her husband of some eight years.

Like a lot of Oxford Dons, Felicity had kept her

maiden name for working purposes and out of a natural (but some said stubbornly feminist) desire to retain her identity.

Now Felicity sighed wearily and straightened up, pushing her long length of wet hair from off of her face and reaching for the soap.

'I didn't think there was,' she lied. 'Sir Laurence was too old, Dr Ngabe is too young to have made much of a dent, and Martha Doyle hasn't done anything good in years.'

'But this Gideon Welles guy,' Clive sneered. 'You never mentioned him, did you?'

'Clive please,' she said wearily.

'You know that money could have dug us out of the hole, don't you?' Clive snarled, whirling away from the shower cubicle and moodily slamming down the toilet seat lid so that he could sit on it and sulk.

Felicity laughed grimly. Did she know? Of course she knew.

If only those investments she'd made two years ago had panned out.

She'd had no illusions about her husband when she'd married him. An out-of-work actor, he was younger than herself, more beautiful than herself, and sexually capricious.

Julie was middle-aged and besotted. To keep him, she knew that she'd need money (plenty of it) and prospects. As an Oxford Don, she'd had the latter. And, in desperation, she'd tried to acquire the former.

Now on the verge of bankruptcy, only the huge amount of cash that came with winning the Van Gilder chair would have kept their heads above water.

She scrubbed herself down vigorously, obsessively, gouging out the tender skin under her fingernails, lathering and washing and lathering again every inch of her body.

'We're going to lose the house, aren't we?' Clive's angry voice cut through the soothing hiss of the water.

They had bought their house in Woodstock Road during the first fall in property prices after the eighties bubble had burst. Now it was worth a lot more than they'd paid for it. It had been a wonderful status symbol, the ultimate in elegant living.

Now…

Felicity Ollenbach continued to weep, bitterly and in private, beneath the disguising spray of the shower.

'No Clive,' she muttered, 'we're not going to lose the house.'

No way were they going to lose the house.

Dr Martha Doyle watched her lover packing. She'd always known he was about to leave her, of course, but tonight was lousy timing even for him!

'Don't slam the door on the way out, you louse,' she said with a viciousness that was more for show, than out of any real hurt.

She felt curiously flat and tired.

'I won't. And so sorry you didn't get that chair, sweetie,' the mocking voice was muffled, as his head rummaged around in the wardrobe.

Martha grunted. 'Old Gideon deserved it, I suppose.'

The man finished his packing and snapped his suitcase shut. He regarded her with a mocking smile and no regrets.

'You suppose,' he mocked. 'Admit it. You're mad enough to spit tin tacks. You've lived your life for a career and that career, after a golden sunburst of promise, has fizzled out like a wet weekend.'

Martha laughed sourly. 'And you have to go now? Abandon me in my hour of need?'

'You know I do. Things to do and people to see.'

'Creep.'

'Bitch.'

Martha watched him go, and then sighed deeply. The apartment suddenly seemed empty.

Her life seemed empty.

It was not, funnily enough, how she had expected to feel. She picked up a shoe and threw it at the door. Down below, in the stairwell, she could hear her lover laugh.

Her ex-lover now she supposed.

She needed a drink!

But still, there were always compensations.

chapter seven

Laurel looked up as Gideon walked in. She was sitting in a large armchair, her legs tucked up under her like a little girl, sipping brandy dispiritedly.

'It's gone, right?' she said flatly.

Gideon nodded. 'I told the Principal. He wants to keep the police out of it. At least for the time being.'

Laurel frowned. 'I don't think I can agree to that,' she said cautiously. Her first instinct was to cover all her bases. And fast.

'He's anxious to avoid bad publicity,' Gideon explained carefully, slumping down in the chair opposite her and putting one foot across his knee. He ran his fingers across his lacerated instep and winced.

Laurel snorted. 'Huh! He doesn't want bad publicity!' she said disgustedly. 'He thinks I do? The last thing I need is to have the Van Gilder name dragged through the mud.'

Gideon looked at her curiously. She sounded her usual fierce and arrogant self all right, but he was sure he'd caught a hint of something else.

Fear?

Yes, perhaps that too, but something else.

Worry.

Yes, she was definitely worried. Instantly, the psychologist in him took over. Slowly, he lowered his foot to the floor and leaned forward in his chair.

'You sound as if you have the weight of the whole world on your shoulders,' he said softly, in his encouraging, questioning voice.

Many times, his students or friends had unburdened themselves after being subjected to just this tone of his voice.

But Laurel, it seemed, was made of different stuff altogether for she merely sighed, then laughed. Wearily she rubbed a hand across her face. 'Poor little rich girl, huh?' she said self-mockingly. Then her eyes sharpened. 'You're bleeding!'

Gideon glanced down at the carpet where she was staring and quickly lifted his feet off the floor. 'Damn!'

'You didn't go out in bare feet!' Laurel squeaked, slipping to her knees in front of his chair and grabbing one ankle.

Gideon just had time to squawk a protest, before she hoisted his leg up and stared at his foot.

'You idiot,' she said. 'Where's the antiseptic cream?'

His ankle felt hot where her fingers were closed around it and he had to swallow – hard – before he told her where the First Aid kit was. He supposed, albeit reluctantly, that it made more sense for her to go and get it, than for him to bleed all over the carpet on the way there and back.

When she returned with a bowl of warm water, a bag of cotton wool and some antiseptic, he firmly took over, refusing to let her minister to him but sinking his feet in the water with a sigh of bliss.

'Are you sure you don't want me to help,' Laurel said, stooping down in front of him, her hand reaching out for his calf.

'No!' Gideon yelped. 'Thanks,' he added as she stood up, her eyes mocking him.

Gideon gritted his teeth. Damn the woman – it was as if she knew he didn't dare have her touch him.

He carefully began dabbing his various scrapes.

'I think Sin-Jun wants the chance to do a little insider

digging,' Gideon said determinedly, steering the subject back on to safer ground. He still felt obliged to try and carry out his Principal's wishes, even if he didn't totally agree with them himself.

'I can understand that,' Laurel sympathised. 'But the thing is,' she muttered, 'will calling in the police not backfire on us all?' she mused out loud, gnawing on her lower lip nervously. 'If we hold back and the chalice isn't recovered and we have to call the police in as a last resort, they'll say it was our fault for not calling them in sooner. No, I can't agree to keeping them in the dark. Surely Sin-Jun has some clout in this town?' she asked, turning on him and glaring at him fiercely.

Gideon sighed. 'Suppose he has.'

'Well? Can't he ask them to keep a lid on this thing. Until the chalice is back?' she demanded.

Gideon threw down a piece of cotton wool and slipped his feet back into his slippers. He stood up, walked carefully into the kitchen to throw the water away, and then came back.

He looked at her steadily for a long while, obviously making his mind up about something.

Laurel, aware of the new tension in the air, stopped her pacing and stared at him.

'What?' she said.

Gideon shook his head. 'Nothing. It's only…'

Laurel took a huge breath. 'Come on, Gideon, just spit it out,' she demanded. 'This is no time for beating around the bush.'

Gideon sat down and looked at her levelly as she retook her seat in the big armchair opposite him. 'I don't know you very well, do I?' he said slowly, and saw that he'd surprised her.

'Well, no, I don't suppose you do,' she said, confusion

making her feel uneasy. 'But what's that got to do with anything?' she asked, with far less aggression in her voice now. Sensing that something was wrong, very wrong, she sat forward, her hands rubbing nervously up and down her knees.

'I've been thinking,' Gideon said.

How much can I trust you?

'Just how did the thief know the chalice was there?'

Laurel opened her mouth, then closed it again. Her eyes sharpened. Suddenly she laughed. It was a hard, biting laugh. 'Oh, I get it. Now I understand why old Sin-Jun is so anxious to keep the cops out of this. It had to be one of your lot, didn't it?' she accused.

Gideon winced. 'Did anyone ever tell you that you have a very crude mouth?' he snapped. But as he spoke, he glanced at her lips and realised, rather abruptly, that as a matter-of-fact she had a very shapely mouth. With a full upper lip and a cupid's bow that begged to be kissed.

'Sure, all the time,' Laurel snapped. 'Did anyone ever tell you that you're as two-faced as…as…'

'Janus?' Gideon named the Roman god that had two faces with a helpful and sweet smile.

Laurel glared at him, then felt a reluctant smile tugging at her lips. She had to hand it to him, the man had class.

'Fine, whatever,' she said. 'Let's face facts. The chalice had to have been stolen by someone at the party tonight, right?'

Gideon shook his head. She was quick this American woman. 'I just can't believe it though,' he said helplessly. 'And yet, I don't see any other way around it. Look, I know I've no right to ask you this, but…' He stopped speaking abruptly, as he realised he was on the verge of begging.

'No, I'm sorry,' Laurel said softly, utterly taking him

by surprise. In an instant, she was by his side, her hand supportively squeezing his shoulder. 'I was forgetting. These people are your friends, aren't they? This college is, well, it's your life I guess.'

Gidcon blinked, staring up at her bemused. One moment she was a snarling, loud-mouthed tigress, the next...more understanding that he possibly had a right to expect.

He swallowed hard.

Laurel brushed the fair silvery hair off his forehead. It was so soft and silky to the touch, and really so amazingly fair. Almost white. It was so sexy.

'I mean, when all's said and done, this thing with the chalice is bad for me, for the Van Gilders, but it's hardly the end of the world,' she murmured, absently twisting a strand of his hair around her finger.

Gideon froze in the chair. His heart-rate soared. He closed his eyes briefly, then snapped them open again.

'I've got the option, if I wanted,' Laurel mused, 'of just pushing it all on to the police and doing a Pontius Pilate – you know, washing my hands of it, and distancing the Van Gilder name as far as possible.'

Her fingers were caressing his scalp, and his skin flushed hot. He could feel it travelling all the way down the back of his neck.'

'But for you, this is an absolute disaster,' she said flatly. 'Isn't it?'

Gideon swallowed hard. 'Yes,' he muttered hoarsely. But, in truth, he'd hardly been listening to her words at all. It was her voice – soft, rich, gentle – that had almost hypnotised him.

She leaned into him, pushing aside his knees to stand closer to him, and tenderly kissed his forehead. 'It'll be all right,' she said softly. And kissed one silvery eyebrow.

'It'll be all right, I promise,' she said again, and kissed the small bridge of his nose. 'It'll be all right,' she whispered, and kissed one of his closed eyelids.

He was shaking now. She could feel it.

'It'll be all right.'

Her lips hovered over his own.

Gideon heaved a great shuddering sigh. It felt so good.

Suddenly his eyes snapped open, spearing her with a bright blue icy light. He reared back.

'For pity's sake woman, leave me alone,' he roared, pushing her away, getting to his feet and walking jerkily to the window. For one insane moment, he'd wanted her to go on and on and never stop!

'I'll be glad to,' Laurel snapped back, hurt to the core and storming towards the door.

Gideon spun around, anguished at the look of pain on her face. 'Don't you get it?' he yelled in frustration. 'I don't need a man-eater in my life right now.'

The moment he said it, he could have bitten off his own tongue. Laurel, her hand on the door handle, froze for one instant then turned slowly back to look at him.

She was hurt and confused and scared and tired, and more than ready to hit right back. Where it hurt most.

'That's quite all right,' she said coolly. 'I don't need a suspected thief in mine.'

Gideon paled. 'What?'

Laurel smiled grimly into his wide, shocked eyes. 'You think you're the only one who can put two and two together, Gideon?' she taunted. 'I was there, too, remember, when your Dean said about the alarm being off,' she reminded him with deadly softness.

But as his eyes widened, she realised with a rush of exasperated tenderness that he'd never even considered the fact that he might be suspected of taking the chalice himself.

'Oh you goof!' she cried, and walked out, slamming the door behind her.

Men! They weren't worth it. They simply weren't worth the hassle.

But by the time she'd caught a taxi and been driven home, she'd come to the conclusion that Gideon Welles probably was worth it.

The question was – what did she intend to do about it?

chapter eight

Gideon walked into the breakfast room opposite the Senior common room and became instantly aware of one of those moments in life when everything suddenly seems to change, but for no discernible reason.

Wrong-footed, he stopped, looking around with a quizzical look on his handsome face. The College Butler was circulating with the toast tray and two scouts were dispensing teapots. The hum of conversation was neither more hushed or avid than usual, so it seemed as if Sin-Jun had been successful in keeping the theft of the chalice a secret.

Everything seemed normal and yet Gideon, for some reason, felt like a stranger to it all, even though for the last decade he'd been taking his breakfast here. The exquisite Edwardian, rounded, oak dining tables, the silver cutlery bearing the college crest, the heavy white tablecloths always freshly-washed and crisply-starched, the faded green flock velvet walls and, dominating the far wall, a huge and beautiful Lely portrait, were all familiar and yet, suddenly, he didn't seem to fit into the scene at all.

As if sensing his plight, Rex Jimson-Clarke half-raised a hand, one little finger beckoning him over to his table. The Theology Don was obviously going to take a service somewhere, for he was dressed in his full clerical regalia, complete with dog-collar and his most severe black suit.

'Rex,' Gideon greeted him quietly, as he drew back one of the matching Edwardian chairs and sat down elegantly.

For such a tall man, Gideon had a grace that complimented the room and many of the female eyes turned in his direction were appreciative.

The College Butler deposited toast on the table and waited patiently for his order. Rex was already half-way through a full English breakfast, but the thought of food revolted Gideon. He murmured something about 'just coffee' and waited until they were once more alone.

'Rex, you were at the party last night. Did anything strike you as odd?'

The Theology Don looked at him in surprise. 'Odd? How do you mean. Blotto? Plenty were that, old man.'

Gideon sighed. How did you go about questioning your friends without letting on what it was all about?

'No. Nothing like that, Rex. I mean, did anyone seem particularly upset. Scared or excited?'

'You mean apart from those who were in a deep blue funk because you snaffled the Van Gilder chair, you mean?' Rex asked, still obviously confused.

Gideon sighed. 'Never mind. Forget it.' It was obvious that if Rex had seen anything obviously suspicious, he'd have said so by now. But then, what had he expected? That the thief would give himself away by a show of nerves or remorse? Get real!

Rex continued to stare at Gideon, his puzzlement slowly turning to worry. 'You all right, Gideon?' he asked quietly. 'You seem a bit...I don't know...off.'

Gideon felt like laughing.

Apart from the fact that he was a suspected thief, had a hell-cat on his tail, and now seemed to be facing some kind of mid-life crisis, he was fine.

Something about the older man's intuition made his stomach lurch unpleasantly. If Rex was noticing a change in him, he was in big trouble. 'Oh, it's nothing, I'm just tired, I suppose,' he said miserably.

With every passing second, he was aware that he was becoming more and more a stranger to these people. These people who had shared his life, his career, his living space, for the last fifteen years.

His unease was nothing, he was sure, to do with a certain loud-mouthed American woman.

It just wasn't.

But something was making him feel cheated, somehow. And worried. For the first time ever, he began to question the direction his life had taken. His commitment to the college. His very way of being.

'Well, I'd best be off. I've got a sermon to deliver and I have to be back here by ten-thirty sharp. Tutorials,' Rex sighed, as if teaching wasn't what Oxford was supposed to be all about.

And once again, Gideon felt a disorientating lurch of unease.

One part of him, the clinical psychologist, understood how something as drastic as a theft was bound to upset and agitate a world within a small, self-contained community like St Bedes. Another, more human part of him, began to feel stifled.

And, suddenly, Gideon understood.

Did he have any real friends here? Any real life?

Laurel Van Gilder had been right all along! When – no, if – the news ever broke about the chalice being stolen, just how supportive or helpful would these people be? And if, for some reason, suspicion should fall on him, would these people rally around and help him, or would they quickly distance themselves so that scandal wouldn't fall on them also?

Gideon knew, realistically, that he'd be a pariah and somehow it shocked him. It shouldn't, of course. He was a big boy now, he knew the score. But still, it made him feel as if he'd been wasting his time here. Letting life just drift on by.

And how much of this had Laurel Van Gilder realised, when she'd stroked his hair last night, offering comfort that he'd then thrown back in her face?

At the time, he'd thought that she had thrown the fact that he was on the suspect list in his face as nothing more than sour grapes. A way to get under his skin.

As if she needed another way!

Now, though, he wondered. Had she realised how lonely he was?

For a whole second, Gideon fought the insane urge to laugh out loud at the absurdity of it all.

One minute his life had been the same as usual, going along at the same contented pace and then, wham. A woman throws herself under his car and his life goes to blazes.

And, worse still, he was beginning to suspect that that might be the best thing that had ever happened to him.

Gideon sighed deeply and reached for the coffee pot. He was overtired and getting the jitters was not going to help him. Neither was feeling sorry for himself.

Clearly, he had to get to the bottom of this affair himself. He didn't know if Laurel had called in the police or not – he wasn't certain what her current state of mind would be like after the debacle last night.

But one thing was for sure – no policeman would know college life, or his colleagues, like he did. They wouldn't have a clue how the colleges operated, or the ins and outs of the academic world.

However, Gideon Welles most certainly did.

But where to start?

With the people at the party, of course. If it wasn't a

random thief who just happened to get very, very lucky, then it had to be someone at the party. And, moreover, there were only a very limited number of suspects.

Sir Laurence. No, that was impossible. Sir Laurence was about to retire, was a pillar of the community and – more to the point perhaps – was wealthy in his own right. He'd have no need to steal a valuable object. Unless he was an avid collector. Collectors, he knew, could be merciless and without conscience when it came to adding to their treasures. But he was sure he'd have known about it if Sir Laurence was a collector of antique silver.

So, who else knew the chalice was there and that the alarm was faulty?

The Psychology Don's high forehead began to wrinkle in concentrated thought.

Martha Doyle.

Gideon shook his head. Slightly promiscuous, good-hearted Martha, a thief? It just wouldn't gel somehow. She was too laid back. Too at ease with herself and her world to risk it by taking such a chance.

Unless she was desperate for money?

That left Doctor Ollenbach and Julie Ngabe.

Gideon knew that Felicity Ollenbach did a lot of television stuff and wasn't that supposed to pay very well indeed?

His thoughts turned thoughtfully to the African woman. Did that serene exterior hide someone who would steal?

It just seemed so outrageous. Next he'd be wondering about the Dean!

Or Sin-Jun!

Gideon wearily rubbed his face. Perhaps he was going about this the wrong way.

He needed something concrete. An indisputable

fact on which to start.

Which was simple.

Whoever it was must have left the party for a short time, to break into the glass cabinet and steal the chalice. Then what? Hide it? Take it home and come back to the party? So, he was looking for someone who'd been missing from the party for five to ten minutes.

Maybe more.

Surely that would narrow it down?

It was also someone who was willing to take a chance on getting caught.

Someone who was desperate enough to try it. For surely it must have been a spur-of-the-minute decision? The thief wouldn't have known it would even be at St Bedes, let alone in a cabinet that was temporarily vulnerable.

No, someone must have acted on sheer inspiration.

Surely it wouldn't be hard to find that someone? And when he did, perhaps he'd find out that whoever it was now heartily sorry they'd even yielded to temptation. It might be possible to get the chalice back without any criminal proceedings at all.

He wondered, grimly, if he was back to living in cloud cuckoo land again. And realised that, whatever happened, his life had now changed irreversibly.

Damn that woman.

She was turning his whole life upside down!

Laurel yawned, rolled over, and cast a baleful eye at the clock. Nearly nine-thirty. It was no use. In spite of not sleeping a wink and feeling raggedly tired, she simply wasn't going to be able to lie in.

She dragged herself out of bed, aching and tired, and stumbled to the shower. The hot water helped a little and she shampooed her hair and towel-dried it, before selecting an amber and bronze suit from her wardrobe. The colour did a lot to emphasise her long black hair and ebony eyes. The autumnal colours looked good on her as she added the merest touch of bronze eyeshadow to her lids, and a muted lipstick to her wide mouth.

At least she looked presentable.

All dressed up and nowhere to go.

She sighed and wandered to the kitchen, making herself coffee and popping some sliced bread into the toaster. She felt restless. Couldn't settle. Couldn't seem to think.

She turned on the radio but, of course, there was no news about the theft at the college.

She'd spent all night wondering whether she should call in the police and then finally decided she wouldn't.

And that had nothing to do with the fact that Gideon Welles would be treated as a suspect. Questioned. Humiliated.

No. That hadn't come into it at all.

Laurel shook her head and met her reflection in the mirror.

'Who are you trying to kid, kid?' she asked herself wryly. 'Oh no!' she said weakly, sinking back in her chair.

It was all so stupid. As if Gideon, that great big oaf, would steal anything!

Laurel marched out into the hall, grabbed her coat, and stepped outside into the damp, foggy morning.

Brown's was crowded, as it always was during the lunch hour. Gideon stepped inside the popular restaurant and glanced around. As he'd expected, Martha Doyle was sitting in her usual corner, her long honey-coloured hair caught back in an elegant chignon.

She saw him come in and her blue eyes gentled. She smiled.

At her own table in the corner, Laurel Van Gilder glanced from behind the huge menu she was hiding behind and noticed the older woman's sudden change of expression.

She'd been busy that morning, making up a list of all those people who knew the whereabouts of the chalice and that the alarm was faulty, and was currently working her way through them, just 'accidentally bumping into them' and talking about the party. It was easy. People so liked to talk about things to the rich and influential.

So far she'd spoken to Rex Jimson-Clarke, having tracked him down at a church in Wolvercote, several of the college scouts who'd been serving that night, as well as three other guests, just trying to get an overall picture of the events of last night from neutral parties.

But, so far, nobody had noticed a thing. Nobody acting out of character, no sound of breaking glass outside the Senior common room, nobody clutching a handbag to their bosom and looking wild-eyed.

Nothing.

It had been one of the scouts who'd told her that Brown's was the place to go if she wanted to talk to academics.

Spotting Martha Doyle, one of the shortlisted candidates for the chair and one of those to overhear about the faulty alarm, had been a major bonus.

But by then she'd been hungry and thirsty and temporarily talked out. She'd opted for a salad and a breather before tackling Dr Doyle.

Now she was glad she had. For unless she mistook the look on her face (and no woman would) Martha was all set to meet a lover.

She glanced across towards the door to see who had put that certain smile on her face and went cold.

Gideon, oblivious to the eyes boring into his back, smiled and walked towards his colleague. 'Martha. Can I join you?'

'Of course love. Any time.'

Gideon smiled. Martha was a notorious and self-confessed flirt. 'Drink?'

'G and T please.'

Gideon ordered, glancing around as he did so. The usual crowd. A host of Dons and Fellows, a smattering of well-heeled undergraduates. Even one or two businessmen, who were definitely in the minority, and someone overwhelmed by the menu over in the corner!

'You look like hell, darling,' Martha said sympathetically. 'Been celebrating a bit hard, have we?'

Gideon nodded. He'd always liked Martha. She was a feminine woman, but also a straightforward, basic, honest woman. Someone he could deal with.

'Yes, something like that,' he lied. Celebrating had been the last thing on his mind last night.

Unaware that the woman hiding in the corner had exceptionally good ears and, although she had to strain, was succeeding quite admirably in listening in on their conversation, he leaned forward resting his elbows on the table.

'Martha, did you speak to Dr Ngabe last night?' he asked casually.

'Julie? No, I don't think so. We also-rans tended to avoid each other if we could.'

Gideon sighed. 'Did you see her leave the party at all, do you remember noticing? For a few minutes? Maybe ten?'

'Not that I can remember,' Martha said. 'Why? Don't

tell me you fancy the luscious lady?'

Gideon smiled and waved a hand. 'How about Dr Ollenbach. Did she leave the party?'

'Sure, I think so. But then, so did you,' Martha said.

'Me? Oh yes, you're right.' He'd gone to the bathroom for a short time. But it proved that Martha had good eyes and noticed things. 'How about Sir Laurence?'

'No. He was button-holed by that little man from Barton Hall. You know the one.'

Gideon winced. 'Oh him.' The Don she was talking about could talk the hind leg off a donkey!

'Poor Sir Laurence never managed to get out until Sin-Jun started to throw us all out.'

So that let Sir Laurence off then.

'Did anyone seem over-excited that you noticed?'

He watched her carefully, but saw nothing even remotely like suspicion or worry cross her face. If she wondered why Gideon was asking her all these questions, she didn't show it.

'No. I thought the Dean looked a bit distracted. But that could have been because he was worried about the alarm. Did he get it fixed, by the way?' Gideon stiffened. Was she hinting at something? A double bluff. Or was she just casually enquiring.

'Oh yes, the man came from London a few hours later.'

He decided not to push his luck and tell her that the chalice wasn't on display right now. Or should he? He leaned forward, the better to watch her reaction. 'Not that it matters. Sin-Jun and Miss Van Gilder decided between them to get the chalice professionally cleaned.'

Martha looked slightly amused, nothing more. 'Really? Looked fine to me.'

But she was obviously disinterested and, in his heart, Gideon couldn't believe she was this good an actress.

He smiled and Martha smiled back. It looked like a very intimate gesture. The gesture of a man who wanted to get closer to his paramour.

She leaned forward slightly herself now, laying a hand across his. 'Let's have dinner tonight,' she said and Gideon flushed, realising she'd been taking all this the wrong way.

'Oh Martha, I...'

She squeezed his hand.

He smiled vaguely. 'Can I take a rain check? I'm up to my ears in exam papers. I'm setting a multiple choice for Prelims.'

Over in her corner, peeping from behind the laminated menu, Laurel gritted her teeth and simmered as she watched the two Dons flirt and play.

Why didn't Martha Doyle just crawl across the table and climb into his shirt whilst she was at it?

'I know how that is,' Martha was saying, wrinkling her nose in sympathy. 'Well, no hard feelings. It's your loss,' she grinned unabashed at him, and Gideon sighed in relief.

The waiter came and he ordered a sandwich which was the speciality of the house and for a while they talked shop. Martha picked his brains for a lecture she was giving at a prestigious American University in Trinity Term, and praised him lavishly on his new book, all the while flirting with him outrageously.

And after his rocky morning he let her, enjoying the repartee and unimportant ego massaging. Eventually they finished their wine and rose to leave.

Outside, Martha hailed a taxi, never liking to walk if she could ride. Gideon watched her go and was about to turn left, back towards college, when he suddenly felt his elbow grabbed.

He turned and looked into furious brown eyes.

'Well, that was a disgusting spectacle,' Laurel snapped. 'And in public too.'

Gideon felt himself blush. 'What on earth! Were you the one who was lurking behind that menu?'

Laurel's chin lifted. 'What if I was?'

'Enjoy playing "I spy" did you?' Gideon jeered.

'As much as you were enjoying playing Sherlock Holmes!' she flashed back.

Again Gideon felt himself flush. What was it about her that could reduce him to little-boy inadequacy?

'Someone's got to find out who took that stupid chalice of yours,' he stated grimly, stiffening his spine and retrieving his dignity.

'I agree,' Laurel said, totally taking the wind out of his sails. 'So I suggest we call a truce and get our heads together.'

'What?' He reared back, his icy blue eyes flaring. 'Oh no!'

He held out his hands as if trying to ward her off. 'Oh no. No, no, no.' His fair head moved vigorously from side-to-side.

Laurel cocked her own head to one side, rather like a robin eyeing a very juicy, appealing worm.

'If you think I'm going to let you drag the Van Gilder chair through the mud, you'd better think again, buddy,' she drawled grimly. 'Until this mess is cleared up, it's you and me. All the way.'

And as she said it, she knew she meant it.

All the way.

All the way.

Oh no, she thought in sudden dismay.

I love the jerk!

chapter nine

Laurel recognised the Morgan at once, of course. How could she ever forget it, after sailing across its bonnet in such a spectacular fashion? Or, after realising the extent of her feelings for its owner, how was she ever likely to forget anything that was even remotely connected with Dr Gideon Welles?

After telling her yesterday that he hadn't needed her help in investigating the missing chalice, she'd let him have the last word and storm off, but only because she'd needed time to regroup herself.

It was a bit of a problem, realising for the first time that you'd fallen flat-out, no-fooling, in love with a man – who probably couldn't stand the sight of you.

But she was not one to let such obstacles stand in her way, and so after moping about the house and getting slightly drunk last night, she'd gone to bed, had a good cry, and then risen that morning in a far more determined frame of mind.

First things first.

She'd cancelled all her other appointments scheduled for her British visit, and would no doubt be hearing from her uncles very soon. But she'd cross that bridge when she came to it.

Her father had never allowed anyone to doubt or threaten his position as head of the show, and she would have to start off as she meant to go on if she were to follow his example.

Which meant that, if she deemed it necessary to stay

in Oxford and safeguard the good name and reputation of the Van Gilder chair, then that's what she'd do. And her family had better go along with her thinking... or else.

Or else what, was something she had not yet got around to working out.

She'd showered and washed her hair, humming defiantly cheerfully as she did so, and dressed in a deep burgundy pair of slacks with a cream and burgundy cashmere sweater. Over that she wore a long grey, sheep-skin-lined coat, and ankle boots of the same colour.

She'd arranged her hair in a loose plait, and left it laying against her spine, where it swung to and fro as she marched confidently down the Woodstock Road towards St Bedes. She'd just reached the main gates, when she had spotted the Morgan pulling out of the narrow alleyway and signal left.

Grimly, before she could pause to think, she quickly ran down the remaining few yards of pavement and stepped firmly into the line of the Morgan's path.

Gideon swore savagely and slammed on the brakes. The angry squeal that came from the classic car caused a few pedestrians to glance their way curiously.

Gideon, from his low bucket seat, glared at her through the windscreen. 'Are you determined to kill yourself by throwing yourself under my car in particular, or will any poor motorist do?' he snapped.

Laurel grinned at him widely. No doubt about it, she'd picked a prime specimen to finally fall in love with. Tall – that was an understatement! – good-looking, very intelligent, and with just a hint of repressed sexuality that she was going to enjoy playing with.

Like handling dynamite.

She took a long, deep breath.

Excitement prickled the air, along with the sharp November frost. All around her, the trees were shedding their leaves. Winter mist teased the fabled dreaming spires, and a winter malaise seemed to be spreading throughout the city as the British resigned themselves to their long, wet, and cold winter.

But Laurel felt only the joys of spring.

Of course, falling in love had not been a good idea under the circumstances. But when did you ever get to choose the time and place?

At first, as she'd stood outside Brown's, gaping at him and reeling under the sudden revelation that she loved him, she'd been inclined to panic.

First, she'd walked home, telling herself that she was mistaken. She was just caught up in the theft and the fraught emotions it generated.

Yeah. Right.

Then she'd tried convincing herself it was only an infatuation. Gideon Welles was the sort of man infatuation was made of, after all. That imperial lofty height. That silver hair and those piercing blue eyes.

The trouble with that was that she was no longer a giddy teenager, mooning over idols.

Eventually, yesterday evening, she'd forced herself to face up to facts. She'd met a man to love. Not a fortune hunter. Not a family-vetted, fully-approved WASP, as advertised by all her friends. But a genuine, complicated, sexy, deeply fascinating man.

Which meant that she was faced with womankind's age old alternatives.

Run or fight.

Running was out of the question.

So it was fight time.

Fight to clear his name first, and free him of this

ridiculous suspicion that he'd fallen under. Then fight to get him into her bed and into her life and, hopefully, one day into a church!

Not that this looked particularly likely right at this moment, she thought wryly, as she contemplated his flashing electric-blue eyes and tight, pinched face.

'Lighten up, Gideon,' she said softly. 'You look fit to blow a gasket. Why don't you try to take it easy more?'

She was worried about what stress could do to a man. Especially her man. She wanted to celebrate their golden wedding anniversary one day. Not watch him have a coronary through stress and overwork in his forties! What was it with English men? Were they all so buttoned-up?

Gideon's eyes widened. What on earth would she come up with next? He couldn't remember the last time someone had spoken to him like that.

But she looked so outrageously vibrant, standing there in bright burgundy, with her long black plait falling past her slim waist.

'Oh, get in,' he snapped. 'It's too early in the morning to pick a fight with you.'

Laurel needed no second bidding and, ignoring the less than gracious offer, she quickly nipped around the car and climbed into the passenger seat.

Like all tall people, she seemed to have to fold herself in the middle to get into the deep bucket seat. It was a slightly disconcerting feeling – as if her knees were heading towards her earlobes. She buckled her seatbelt and glanced across at him. He was even taller than she was. How on earth did he manage to drive this thing?

Very well, she soon found out.

Although they never left the confines of the city, and he kept strictly and scrupulously to the speed limit, she could tell he handled the car like a superb craftsman and could well imagine the paces he'd put the sports car through when out on the open country roads. Gear changes were smooth, rapid, and easy. His hands on the steering wheel were light but firm. His eyes seemed to be everywhere at once. Despite being so low to the ground and so exposed to the elements, she felt completely safe.

Suddenly, she realised how lucky she'd been the day she'd crashed her bike into this car. Anyone else might not have had the reactions to brake so quickly. She could have been squished! She shuddered at the thought.

The cold wind whistled over the tops of their heads as they headed up Woodstock Road, further into the affluent, leafy suburbs of north Oxford.

'Where are we going?' she asked at last.

'Dr Ollenbach's.'

'Why?'

He glanced at her briefly. 'Why do you think?'

Laurel was glad there was no condescension in his voice. Some very clever people had a nasty habit of presuming everyone else was of lesser intelligence. But his voice had been encouraging more than anything. More interested to hear her response.

Laurel didn't need long to think it through. 'Do you think she's just gonna come across and say, "Oh yeah, sure, I pinched your bit of silver"?'

Gideon just had to grin. She had such a turn of phrase. 'No.'

'Oh. So you think she might have some idea who might have pinched it and tell you all about it?'

Gideon glanced across at her. 'Can you get serious for a moment?'

'Sure.'

'Right. First off – have you called in the police yet?'

'No. I thought I'd give St Bedes and Sin-Jun a bit of a

break. Mind you,' she added hastily, as he breathed a sigh of relief, 'I'm not going to sit on this thing forever. If we're no farther forward by the end of the day, I might have to call them in.'

Gideon nodded, indicated and overtook a fume-belching city bus, and then pulled back into his lane. 'Fair enough. Now, second question. Do we tell anyone that the chalice is missing?'

Laurel cocked her head to one side and regarded him thoughtfully. He had a marvellous profile. Strong straight nose, firm chin. High forehead and a big wave of near-white hair.

'Laurel?'

'Huh? What? – oh no. I mean, why would we tell anyone that the chalice has been stolen. I thought you and Sin-Jun were hot to keep it a nasty little secret.'

'We do. But I've been thinking.'

'Something I know you do so well.'

'Don't get snippy!'

'I wasn't!' Laurel fumed. 'I meant it. It was a compliment. What is it – can't you take one off a woman? Or are you just not used to them?'

Gideon gave her a quick, slightly appalled, glance and mumbled an apology.

Laurel hid her grin.

'So, you were saying,' she said, mollified. It was nice to know she could handle him. Not that she'd had any doubts, but a girl in her situation needed all the bonuses she could get.

'Yes. I was saying,' Gideon cleared his throat and shifted uncomfortably in his seat. Why did she have to lean so close against him?

'Er, yes. We can hardly go around investigating the disappearance without giving some explanation can we?

I mean, when I questioned Martha yesterday, she wasn't really paying much attention. Martha's the sort who wouldn't. But the doctors – Ollenbach and Ngabe – are going to be very different.'

Laurel sniffed. She didn't want to think about the flirtatious, ripe, Martha Doyle.

Still, she saw he had a point. 'Right. We can't just waltz in and demand to know what they did when they left the party. And, by the way, all you shortlisted people, except for Sir Laurence, left the party at some point that night,' she said somewhat smugly.

Gideon refused to be impressed. 'Yes, I know.' He hadn't, however, been able to think of a way of asking Martha just what she'd been doing when she'd left the party for a few minutes.

He was pretty sure, anyway, that she'd done what he'd done – visited the bathroom. Definitely not something he'd ever ask a lady about!

Not that he could imagine Laurel Van Gilder baulking at asking such a question.

He looked across at her with a funny kind of smile on his face. 'I daresay you could come in quite useful after all.'

Laurel flushed. 'Gee, thanks.'

'So what do you think?'

'About my being useful?' she asked archly.

'No. About telling people that the chalice is gone. After all, it can only be Dr Ollenbach or Dr Ngabe, can't it? Sir Laurence never left the room, and I know I didn't take it.'

'You're leaving out your precious Martha.'

'Hell,' Gideon said. He had too. 'OK. So it's Martha, or one of the two others. The thing is, what do we tell them?'

As he spoke, he indicated and pulled up outside a large, comfortable looking, white-fronted villa. Laurel sighed. 'You're right. We've got to tell them about the missing chalice, otherwise they're not going to answer any questions. And it's not as if we'll be telling the guilty party something they don't already know. In fact, I guess they'll be wondering why it isn't in all the papers by now.'

Gideon smiled. 'I doubt it. They'd know the college would instantly go into damage limitation mode.'

Laurel nodded. 'So, yes. We tell them we're investigating the theft. On the quiet, before the police are called in.'

Gideon noticed that she didn't hold out much hope that the guilty party would have a fit of remorse and offer to give the chalice back.

'But will they keep quiet about it? The innocent ones, I mean,' she asked curiously.

'I expect so,' Gideon said. 'They won't want to be associated with it in any way at all. In Oxford, your reputation is all that matters. How many books you've written, and how well the critics received them. What lecture tours you get invited on. Who you know. What you know. And never having a breath of scandal breathed on you. That's all that matters. Not money, not looks, not personality. Your whole life depends on your academic performance and personal reputation. Divorce can still damage a person here, if it's messy or scandalous. And a college like St Bedes, with a big theology school, is even more jealous of its staff's behaviour than most. If people get even a whiff of things not being quite right, students suddenly stop wanting to attend your tutorials, your lectures, your college. People begin to talk. The rumour mill gets going. People – important people – begin to feel embarrassed by being associated with you and, when that happens, Principals look for ways to get rid of you. Then it's down the drain time. Oh yes. Everyone will keep quiet all right – guilty and innocent alike.'

Laurel, listening to him, had gone pale. 'I had no idea you lived such a precarious life-style. I thought you had it pretty cosy, in fact.'

Gideon, who had it very cosy indeed, felt himself flushing. Then wondered why he should feel so guilty. It was hardly his fault if he was a blameless high-flyer!

Grumpily, he got out of the car, unaware that Laurel watched his unfolding, swinging out, and rising, all in one lithe graceful movement, with open-jawed admiration and envy. She herself had to struggle to get up and clamber out, feeling a bit like a cannon ball trying to squeeze through the mouth of a milk bottle.

She shut the car door, grumbling under her breath. The Morgan was going to have to go!

Why couldn't he drive a Rolls Royce like anyone else with any sense? But as she slammed the car door behind her, and looked down at the crouching green car, she couldn't help but admire the rounded look of it, the old, utterly British elegance of the thing.

And Gideon did look so spectacular in it. Well, perhaps the Morgan could stay.

She suddenly laughed at herself. Who was she kidding? Hell, she'd give him anything, promise him anything, if only he'd take her in his arms and kiss her again.

How silly, how ludicrous, to be so utterly in love with a man who'd only kissed her once. No. Correction. She'd kissed him, as she recalled. And he hadn't been too pleased about it.

She suddenly snapped to, as she realised he was looking at her quizzically. 'Are you going to stand there day dreaming all day or are you coming inside?' he asked, with definite condescension in his voice now.

Laurel smiled grimly. 'Hah! I'd like to see you question the good Felicity Ollenbach all by yourself. She'd have you tied in knots in ten seconds flat.'

Gideon watched her march past him, head in the air, plait tossing pertly against her rump, and took a deep breath.

Laurel pressed the doorbell aggressively and took a step back.

The house was set in a large expanse of ground, neatly tended by a professional gardener by the looks of it. The window panes and paintwork had been recently painted. 'Very nice,' she murmured. 'This place must be worth at least…'

The door opened abruptly. Laurel, who had been planning to use a hearty, all-American-girls-together approach, found herself unexpectedly thwarted.

For on the doorstep stood a young, very handsome man, with a very shapely but petulant looking mouth, a head of curly brown hair, and deep-set, appealing grey eyes.

'Oh,' she said blankly.

'You must be Mr Ollenbach?' Gideon, sensing her sudden confusion, put in smoothly.

'No. Yes. I mean, I am Felicity's husband, but my name is Westlake. So is hers, if she thought it was good enough to use. Which she obviously doesn't.'

There was a short, appalled silence.

What a louse, Laurel thought. Bad mouthing his wife in front of complete strangers. If I were Felicity, I'd soon tell this clown where to get off.

Gideon, however, had a far more professional reaction to the sneering statements.

There was obviously some deep-rooted resentment towards his wife's success, he thought clinically. Which meant that he must be insecure in his own professional life. He wondered if the man was a manual labourer, but a quick look at his hands showed him this was not the case.

He'd also been drinking, Gideon noticed, the medic rather than the psychiatrist in him recognising all the telltale signs. 'Is your wife at home?' he asked politely, carefully not calling her by the name of Ollenbach. No point antagonising him any further.

'Sure she is. Though she's off to the brain mill before long.'

Gideon, who knew Dr Ollenbach's college fairly well, wondered what the Dean of that august house would think of his establishment being referred to as a 'brain mill'.

Laurel stepped inside first, looking around. Nice chandelier, definitely authentic. A few good paintings, but not spectacular ones. The mirror was Venetian.

All in all, an impressive hallway. But a careful one. Money, she mused, was tight. But they didn't want anyone to know that. Interesting.

Gideon, on the other hand, barely glanced around. He was too busy studying the handsome young man who, with obvious ill grace, was leading them into a charming study-cum-library-cum-den, at the rear of the house. The one big window overlooked a large garden, and a high wall surrounded the property.

'Flick. Visitors.'

Dr Felicity Ollenbach was sitting on a large leather sofa and she rose slowly, a puzzled look on her face.

'Professor Welles. Miss Van Gilder. How nice.'

'Welles?' the sharp, ugly-toned voice, came from

Clive Westlake.

Gideon, looking from his colleague to her spouse, suddenly realised the large age difference that existed between them. He felt an unexpected shaft of pity for Felicity. Then he felt an equally nasty jolt of shame.

Who was he to instantly jump to conclusions?

'So you're the jammy creep who won the chair,' Clive said, swaggering over to the sofa and flopping down into it. Something in the boneless way he did it made Laurel blink. It was barely nine o'clock in the morning, but the man was already drunk!

The atmosphere in the room was as ugly as a pea-soup fog in an industrial complex.

'Yes, I won the Van Gilder chair,' Gideon admitted levelly. He looked in apology at his colleague.

He could see the agony and apprehension shining in her eyes, although she was using every trick in the book to hide it. She was carefully monitoring her body language, forcing herself to sit back down, imitating a woman at ease with herself and the world.

Once again, he felt a shaft of pity assail him. 'I'm sorry, this is obviously a bad time to call,' he said and made backward shuffling movements towards the door.

For the first time since he started this crusade, he began to realise what investigating a sensitive theft actually entailed.

It wasn't all going to be clues and deduction. It meant grubbing around in peoples lives.

Laurel shot him a half-angry, half-loving look. Just as she thought. Putty in a woman's hands.

'Hello Mr Westlake, we haven't been properly introduced,' Laurel attacked the obvious weak link in the chain with one of her brightest smiles. 'I'm Laurel Van Gilder.'

She walked forward and held out her hand. Clive smiled nastily and deigned to take it.

'Oh yes,' he drawled and held on to her fingers, insolently rubbing them suggestively with his own. Laurel kept her smile firmly in place, even as her flesh crawled. 'You're the woman who gave him the chair. How nice of you.'

Laurel slowly withdrew her hand. 'Actually, Mr Westlake, I didn't give him anything,' she said sweetly. 'An independent board of academics voted on who was to be awarded the chair and then informed me of their decision. I merely handed over the prize.'

'And all that money,' Clive added. But there was a bitter tone of angst in his voice now, over-riding that of sneering loathing. Felicity cast him an agonised look.

Gideon, in that moment, understood it all. It was not the loss of prestige that mattered here. It was the loss of the money that went with it.

An academic could make a lot of money, or very little. And he knew from experience, even those who earned huge fees, very often invested it badly. How many of his friends, brilliant in their own fields, were hopeless at handling money?

'Is that so?' Clive Westlake, mercifully unaware of the other man's pity, was still concentrating his attention on Laurel.

It was easier than dealing with Gideon Welles.

Like all handsome men who had to rely on their looks, Clive didn't like being in the presence of one who's physicality outshone his own.

Not that that silver-haired, freakish giant was in any way good-looking, of course, he thought complacently. But the American babe really was a looker.

'Of course, the fact that you and Professor Welles

obviously get on so well together has nothing to do with it. Hum?' he drawled suggestively.

Laurel laughed. It cut Clive down to size like nothing else could. 'I first met Professor Welles at the prize-giving,' she lied superbly. 'But I must say, Dr Ollenbach, that after meeting you, I was rather hoping that it was your name in the envelope after all. I was feeling a bit surrounded by all those Englishmen.'

Felicity managed a smile. 'Oh, we Americans can hold our own.'

'Come to gloat, have you Professor Welles?' Clive once more turned the atmosphere nasty.

'Clive!' Felicity cried.

'No,' Gideon said quietly. 'We came to ask you, Felicity, if you saw anything at the party that might help explain a rather unfortunate incident that occured some time that night.'

'Aye? What's this?' Clive demanded, before his wife could say a word.

'I'm afraid the Augentine chalice that comes with the chair for the duration, was stolen,' Laurel said. 'The same night of the party. In fact, while the party was going on.'

She was looking at Clive, Gideon at Felicity. Both of them went pale and looked bewildered.

But whereas Felicity began to look apprehensive, her husband began to bluster.

'Is that how you egg-heads describe theft, is it? An unfortunate incident?'

'Were you at the party, Mr Westlake?' Laurel put in sweetly. 'I'm sure I would have remembered seeing you there.'

'No,' Felicity said quickly. 'Clive had an audition. He had to go to the playhouse to read for a part.'

So he was an actor, Gideon and Laurel thought simultaneously. That, perhaps, explained quite a lot.

'Did you get it?' Laurel couldn't resist asking, because she'd already guessed the answer. Clive's very unlovely flush confirmed her suspicions.

'No,' he said shortly.

'And I'm afraid I can't help you either,' Felicity said, with a touch of asperity. 'I saw nothing unusual. And why should I? A thief was hardly likely to gatecrash the party, was he?'

Laurel recognised Felicity's loyalty to her man, and felt a bit guilty for taking pot shots at him.

She gave herself a stern reminder to stick to the facts. 'We were wondering if you saw anything unusual when you left the party. You were gone for about ten minutes or so, weren't you? Around eleven-fifteen, I believe it was,' she said calmly.

Felicity started. 'How did you…well, I…no.'

'What on earth is this?' Clive broke in. 'What are you implying?'

'We're not implying anything,' Gideon cut in. 'We're just trying to get to the bottom of this before calling in the police.'

Felicity paled even further. But then, that meant nothing Gideon realised. Hadn't he just explained to Laurel how being mixed up, even if you were innocent, in a police matter would be something for any Don to fear.

Clive looked uneasily from the two visitors to his wife. 'I don't get it,' he said slowly. 'I think you two ought to leave.'

'Where did you go, Dr Ollenbach?' Laurel said quietly but firmly.

'Outside for some air. I walked around the Fellows

Garden for a bit. Those weeping silver birches are quite something to see in the moonlight. I had a drink with me. To be quite honest, I was rather disappointed at not winning the chair. I just wanted a few minutes to myself. I didn't notice anything wrong. The last time I saw the chalice, it was when we were coming back from Hall.'

Her voice trailed off. No doubt she was remembering the Dean's loud voice despairing over the faulty alarm.

She looked at Gideon with blank eyes. 'I didn't take it.'

'Do you have any idea who might have done?' he asked softly. He was hating this. Hating it.

But Felicty shook her head. 'I'm afraid not.'

'And you didn't see anything suspicious?' Gideon asked.

'And you saw nothing at all out of the ordinary?' Laurel pressed relentlessly at the same time.

Dr Ollenbach smiled at her grimly. 'I wasn't in a "noticing" sort of mood.'

Clive shifted restlessly on his seat and thrust out his chin belligerently. 'Here, who do you think you are? Miss Marple and Hercule Poirot?' he sneered, laughing at his own joke of comparing a huge man like Welles with the short, fat, bald Agatha Christie detective.

'No, but let's hope we're as successful as they are. Or else it's the police, I'm afraid,' Gideon said, looking at Clive who flushed.

'Well, if you think of anything…' Gideon said. 'Oh, by the way. I don't suppose you took any pictures of the party?'

'No, I didn't have a camera,' Dr Ollenbach said.

'But someone did,' Laurel said, suddenly remembering a man dressed in a dinner suit who'd been happily snapping away. She described him to Gideon, who thought he might be a Philosophy Don invited by the Principal.

'We'll call on him, see if he's got them developed yet,' Gideon said as Felicity, obviously relieved to be able to get up and show them to the door, accompanied them out.

Her husband, mercifully for all concerned, stayed seated. Probably too drunk to get up, Laurel thought waspishly.

At the front door, they said somewhat stilted goodbyes and Dr Ollenbach closed the door after them.

Once back in the car, Laurel glanced across at Gideon. 'My house is just up a few hundred yards here. Do you want to stop for elevenses?'

'Why not?' he agreed tiredly.

He was not surprised to discover that her house was a plush villa, even bigger and better than the Ollenbach residence.

This time Laurel got out of the car with a little more feminine dignity. Practice, they said, made perfect.

Inside, she led him straight to the kitchen, watching him pull out a chair and lean his elbows on the table. She liked his presence, here in her own 'space'. He seemed to fill it just right. Not too much that it threatened to swamp her own existence and personality, but enough to make a substantial difference.

She made him tea and cut him a slice of store-bought cake. She was no pastry chef.

'Well, what do you make of them?' she asked, when they were finally sitting opposite each other in the cosy kitchen.

'I think they're in financial trouble,' he said flatly.

'The house is probably mortgaged to the hilt,' she agreed thoughtfully. 'And that husband must be a millstone around her neck. But she loves him. Poor cow.'

Gideon winced. 'You have a real way with words.

Anybody ever tell you that?'

Laurel grinned at him. 'I might not have the long, fancy-sounding mumbo-jumbo psychological babble you have at your fingertips, Professor Welles, but I know what's what.'

Gideon thought of his own pity for Felicity Ollenbach and wondered if, perhaps, Laurel's way wasn't the more honest.

He sighed. 'I can imagine that husband of hers having sticky fingers,' he admitted glumly.

'She was gone from the party, she admitted as much,' Laurel pointed out.

His eyes flashed blue electricity at her. 'Well? So was I, that doesn't mean anything.'

'You just don't want it to be her, or any of them. Admit it,' Laurel said.

Gideon sighed and shook his head. 'You're right,' he admitted simply. 'I don't.'

'But the Ollenbach house isn't far away from the college is it? If she had her car with her, it would only have taken her a few minutes to drive home, drop the chalice off, and nip back. That way, even if someone noticed the chalice was gone right away and instituted a search, it wouldn't be found.'

Gideon eyed her uneasily. She was like a human dynamo. He got up and rinsed off his plate and cup.

Laurel watched him with approval. Well, at least he was house-trained! She got up and sidled over to him. He was so tall. So slender. So silver. And he smelt good. Just standing next to him was a thrill.

'Don't worry. We're being as tactful as we can. We're doing a good job,' she reassured him softly. 'I don't want to upset your friends. I know you have to live with these people,' she added gently. 'But we have to get the chalice back, or your friends will be hurt even more.'

Surprised at her understanding, he looked down at her. She smiled. 'You really think me a bit of an idiot, don't you?'

'No!' he instantly denied. Her eyes were dark, like the darkest of chocolate. He swayed, leaning a little closer to her. She seemed to be pulling him down to her. How on earth did she do that?

Laurel wasn't about to look a gift-horse in the mouth. 'It'll be all right, you know,' she said softly, standing closer, their arms rubbing against each other now. 'We'll get to the bottom of all this and then…'

Their lips met. Gideon felt his head implode. All thoughts of the outside world vanished. Everything in him was suddenly, in the wink of an eye, concentrated on this one moment, this one sensation.

Sensation of woman.

In his arms, warm, soft, pressing closer, always closer. The scent of her. The soft whispering sound of her breathing. The touch of her tongue, velvet soft, exploring, forcing its way into his mouth and dragging out his soul.

He heard a soft tiny moan of pleasure, but couldn't tell whether it came from her or from himself.

He felt her breasts pressing hard against his, her nipples digging into his ribs. Her leg shifted, pressing against him, against the hardness of his loins, which were stirring, aching, yearning towards the softness of her womanhood.

He tried to take a breath, but couldn't. He just inhaled more of her deeper into him. Her touch. Her smell. Her sound.

He closed his eyes and felt himself sinking to the floor. Cold tiles against his back. Her weight on top of him.

Laurel stretched out over him, luxuriating in touching

him in every part she could. If only she could melt into him.

Their kiss deepened, became ravaging, needing, raging.

Her lips left his at last, but only to travel down to his throat. She pressed her lips to the hollow at the base of his neck, causing him to take a deep, desperate gulp of air…desperately striving for common sense, but also fearing it. He didn't want to be sensible. Not now. Not when she was touching him so closely. He'd been too sensible for too long.

Her hands were on his cheeks, lowering to trace the columns of his taut neck, moving down over his chest, exploring the well-muscled contours of his chest. Down further, to press against his jeans, exploring, fondling, rubbing, the hard bulge there. He pulsated and jumped against her hand.

Gideon had no doubt this time about who was groaning. His own deep voice, hoarse with pleasure, echoed back from the white kitchen walls.

His eyes snapped open.

He was lying on a kitchen floor, beneath a woman who was driving him insane with sexual desire. He should do something!

Her hands pushed up his sweater, her fingers feverishly unbuttoning his shirt. A moment later, her soft hands were moving enticingly over his chest, causing him to writhe helplessly against the hard tiles.

That was it. Enough. He *must* do something!

As she leaned forward to press her lips to his chest, his silvery-gold head thrashed from side-to-side against the black-and-white tiles. He moaned. A needy desperate sound of longing.

'Laurel,' he said her name. Tried to give it shape

and definition. But he saw only sharp cheekbones, huge dark chocolate eyes, a warm, loud, accented voice. Beauty. Strength. Fire.

Laurel's questing fingers were at his belt buckle now. And, suddenly, he somehow found the strength to move, to snap the invisible chains that had seemed to hold him prisoner. He closed his fingers over hers, halting her in mid-motion.

Her hot dark eyes looked up into his face, questioning.

'What are you doing?' he asked hoarsely.

'Making love to you.'

'Why?'

'Because I want to.'

Gideon shook his head. 'Not enough.'

Laurel tensed, sensing a sudden trap. This love thing was new territory to her. Much as she might try to feign confidence, inside she was quivering. 'What else do you want?' she asked coldly. 'You want me to say I love you?'

Because I do.

But she was not going to be the first to say it. No way. She wasn't that suicidal.

Her words acted like a bucket of cold water. Gideon struggled up, coming to the surface, fighting clear the sensual sea of desire that was threatening to drown him.

'Don't be ridiculous,' he snapped, scrambling to his feet, his body cursing him, his head jeeringly applauding his self control. 'We hardly know each other.'

Laurel, too, rose shakily to her feet. Her body, still moist and warm and prepared for invasion, suddenly cooled and calmed and ached.

'That's truc,' shc agreed coolly.

Gideon walked to the sink and slowly leaned over it. He felt wretched. Stupid.

Why couldn't he just have accepted the sex and then

forgotten it? Men did it all the time. He'd done it himself in the past.

But with this woman, somehow he'd known it would be impossible. His subconscious must have known it all the time.

Hooray for his know-it-all subconscious, he thought sourly. 'Look,' he turned to her, running a hand across his pale, sweating, miserable face. His heart was still thundering. His skin could still feel the imprint of her fingers.

He drew a ragged breath. 'Let's just keep this strictly business, all right?'

Laurel smiled. 'Fine by me,' she lied, shrugging one shoulder nonchalantly.

'Right. We'll get to the bottom of all this and then we can part friends,' he pressed, not trusting her sudden compliance.

Why wasn't she spitting and trying to scratch his eyes out?

Laurel smiled. In a pig's eye, she thought inelegantly. Once they'd got to the bottom of all this, then it was open season on Psychology Dons, buddy!

And she'd get him into her bed, kicking and screaming if she had to!

chapter ten

Gideon drove north through the early afternoon traffic. Beside him, Laurel was ominously quiet.

Gideon coughed nervously. In his mind's eye, he could still see himself on her kitchen floor, his body on fire with passion and desire.

How on earth was he supposed to get past that?

Some psychologist he was.

Of course, by far the best thing to do was to get themselves back on an even footing again. Act normal. He cleared his throat.

'I suppose as soon as all this mess is cleared up, you'll be going back to the States?' he asked, with a determined effort at polite conversation.

Laurel shrugged. 'Not right away. I have to go to London and soothe some ruffled feathers down there. One of my uncles is having some trade union problems with one of his UK divisions. Then I have to go up to Scotland to preen some feathers. One of my other uncle's companies has just won a big ship-building contract. Not to build a big super liner, of course,' she carried on knowledgably, 'those contracts go to Sweden and other such places nowadays. But they've won a yacht-building contract. You know, providing status symbols to the *nouveau riche*. Very profitable. Then I have to go over to France – my third uncle has just brought a large perfume enterprise. I daresay they want to name a perfume after me, or get me to agree to a big advertising campaign. But first they have to see if I'm beautiful enough.'

She spoke so matter-of-factly, that Gideon took his eyes off the road for just a scant second to glance across at her. She was looking out of the window, with no visible expression of scorn on her face.

'You're serious, aren't you?' he said, with something approaching awe in his voice. How many women did he know who could be so detached about their appearance? Not many.

Laurel, too, was struggling to act normal. Not because she wanted to forget that morning – hell, she could still feel him beneath her.

For an iceman, he'd felt surprisingly warm. No, it just made things easier not to imagine herself making love to him all the time.

She dragged her thoughts back to the here and now. 'Of course I'm serious,' she said candidly. 'A new perfume launch can cost millions and make millions more. Providing you get the packaging and promotion right. And glamorous women sell perfume – it's sometimes as simple as that. Just think of all the famous movie queens who have their own fragrances. The French company want to make their takeover by an American company sound and look like a good thing. If they think I'm a glamorous enough American heiress figure, who'll appeal to the buying public, they'll want to make use of me. At least, that's what my uncle seems to think although he didn't say so in so many words.'

Gideon sighed. 'Just how many uncles do you have?'

'Three. They all have a different slice of the Van Gilder pie.'

'And your father?'

'My father died not so long ago.'

Gideon's jaw clenched. 'I'm sorry.'

'So was I,' Laurel said simply.

'And where did he fit into the Van Gilder pie?'

'He owned it.'

Gideon swallowed. 'Oh.' It was hard for him to imagine so much wealth.

'Or at least, he appeared to own it. Which, in America, amounts to the same thing,' Laurel amended. 'He was the visible fountainhead – the smiling face of Van Gilder Enterprises.'

Briefly, she explained how her father was the playboy with a heart, the charity worker, the handsome man-about-town.

'Didn't he find that role a bit…' Gideon struggled for the right word, but couldn't find one that wouldn't sound patronising.

'Empty?' Laurel supplied him with one dryly. 'Sometimes. But then, he brought in the contracts that his younger brothers converted into dollars. He played golf with the senators and industrialists who greased the machinery that allowed Van Gilder Enterprises to get the zoning they needed, etc. What my father did was every bit as important as what my uncles do.'

'But who's going to do that now?'

'I am.'

Gideon felt the car swerve a little and grimly fought for control. He pulled up in front of the block of flats and switched off the engine, turning to look at her more fully.

'That's a lot of responsibility,' he said softly.

Laurel shrugged one shoulder. 'He left me the shares. He left me the legacy. This is one little rich American heiress who's going to have to work for her multi-millions.'

Gideon heard just a touch of anxiety in her voice. Hell, if he'd been in her position, there'd be more than a touch of it in his own voice! Suddenly he began to see this affair from her point of view.

Laurel caught the look in his eye. 'What?' she asked softly.

Gideon shook his head. 'Nothing. It's just…presenting the Van Gilder chair. It was your first public appearance as the new Van Gilder figurehead, wasn't it?'

Laurel's lips twisted. 'Yes. And look what a flying start I'm off to.'

Gideon sighed. 'I had no idea it meant so much to you. I thought you were just being pushy.'

Laurel laughed. 'Gee. Thanks. But it's my job to me to handle the publicity, which is why I have to see this through. If I can't do something so simple as hand out an academic award without fluffing it…'

'Hey, hey,' he said softly. 'It isn't your fault that some thief took the chalice,' he pointed out quietly. 'So far, the papers haven't even mentioned the Van Gilder chair, except to give the usual little dry piece about it.'

'I know. But it can all blow up in my face,' Laurel said anxiously. And then, totally out of the blue, she blurted out miserably, 'I miss my father. I miss him so much!'

Gideon nodded. 'I know. Grieving takes a lot longer than most people think. I know just how you feel.'

Laurel looked at him angrily. 'Oh yeah?' False sympathy was not something that she could easily take.

Gideon looked at her steadily. 'Yes, I do. I lost both my parents in an accident when I was a student at St Bedes. One moment I was a nineteen-year-old with a family and a home to go to. The next – it was all gone.'

Laurel felt herself go white. She didn't know how she could have coped if she'd lost her mother too. And her home. She bit her lip. 'Is that why St Bedes is so important to you?'

Gideon blinked. Funny, he hadn't thought about it like that. And it was so obvious really. A psychological classic. Lose one family, seek out another. He smiled ruefully. 'I suppose so.'

Laurel sniffed back the tears that were threatening to swamp her. 'Then it's my turn to say sorry. I thought you were just another stuck-up Brit. One who lived in an Oxford college as a way of showing the world what a wonderful, clever, privileged, superior person he was.'

Gideon shifted uncomfortably in his seat. 'I had no idea that I came across like that.'

'You don't. Not really,' she said quickly. 'It's just that I saw the whole package and didn't think to look beyond it. I'm sorry. I'm sure you love St Bedes just as much as I love my own home.'

Gideon thought back to the moment when he'd walked into the breakfast room yesterday. Or was it the day before? Time seemed to have lost its axis somehow. He remembered how odd the room had looked. How out-of-place he'd felt.

'I wonder,' he mused, making her look at him curiously. Could it possibly be time to move on? Had he become trapped in St Bedes like a well-kept fly preserved in expensive, protective amber? If he had to cope in the real world, in Laurel's cut-throat world, just how well would he fare?

Suddenly, he felt restricted. Before he'd become determined to be a teacher, he'd had other worthy ideals and ambitions – as befitted the very young and naïve.

He'd started off as an undergraduate intending to go into the field of practising psychiatry. And not just tending to the common neurosis of the rich either. But serious, meaningful work with the mentally ill. What had happened to that idealistic dream?

He shook his head. One thing at a time. Find the chalice first. Then have a mid-life crisis!

He noticed that she was looking at him quizzically. He sighed. 'You've got me doubting myself,' he said honestly.

And doubting his own assessment of her too. A spoilt rich brat?

Somehow, he didn't think so. Not any more. She had her problems, just like he did. She had her responsibilities to family. To a life-style. Just like everyone else.

Laurel, too, felt as if they'd somehow just crossed a bridge. She wasn't quite sure how, but she knew instinctively that they were no longer two people on a collision course, but two people in a relationship.

A relationship. What a scary word that was!

Laurel sighed deeply and wearily brushed the long hair off her face. It was at times like these that she missed having her father to talk to. To advise her. To tell her that everything was going to be all right. Ridiculous of course. She was a grown woman, for heaven's sake.

Gideon looked briefly across at her, a worried frown creasing his brows. He, too, wanted to brush the hair from her face, perhaps stroke her cheek, and say something profound.

Something to help.

Instead he said helplessly, 'You look tired. I hope you're getting enough sleep.'

Laurel gave a harsh laugh. 'Hardly, with all this going on. I'm beginning to wonder if we're ever going to get out of this mess,' she added drearily. And wondered if she was talking about the missing chalice – or something else entirely.

Gideon glanced at the nearly deserted road, slowed his speed even more, then reached across to give her hand a quick squeeze before starting the car again. It was, in many ways, a clumsy gesture, but a curiously and deeply touching one also. Laurel felt absurdly comforted and just a little amused.

'Don't worry. Things will work out,' he said, wondering if he could possibly sound more trite if he tried. 'With you around calling the shots, they wouldn't dare do anything else.'

'Huh, don't you believe it,' Laurel laughed. 'I don't know where you've got this idea from that I've got life all pegged,' she huffed.

Gideon grinned widely. 'No, I can't think where I got it from either. Perhaps it's the way you always expect to get what you want – and get it. Or the way you seem able to take life by the throat and shake it – just like a terrier with a rat.'

'Thanks a lot! Are you calling me a dog?' she teased.

Gideon laughed too. 'Certainly not. And if I was, you'd be a French poodle with a diamond collar, dyed fashionably pink, and cut and bobbed in the very latest pom-poms.'

'Oh shut up. I'd be a little shivering ball of fluff looking for a kind master.'

'Oh yeah. I'd bet you've never been a shivering little ball of fluff in your entire life,' he scoffed.

And although she knew he was having fun with her, something about the certainty in his voice cut her on the raw.

'Then you'd be wrong,' she said flatly. 'I've had my share of fear and disappointment, believe me. Once, when I fell off a swing in the school playground when I was five, I broke my leg. But I was so shocked and it hurt so much, that I couldn't even call out to my friends for help. They just went right on playing all around me, whilst I tried to pretend nothing was the matter. It wasn't until the teacher called us in and I didn't even move, that he came over and found out what had happened. I was taken to the hospital but, although it was only an hour or so before they located my mother and she came to get me, it felt like years, believe me.'

Gideon's hands tightened on the steering wheel. He knew just how damaging childhood traumas could be. He wouldn't be surprised if she still had nightmares about it, even now.

'I bet you had all the doctors and nurses jumping through hoops though,' he challenged her softly.

Laurel grinned. 'Well, just a little bit. Then there was…' she hesitated for a fraction of a second, wondering if she really wanted to do this, then plunged on grimly, '…my first love.'

Gideon's eye sharpened on her for a moment, then he very carefully turned his attention back to the road. He knew that keeping his head turned away from her would make her feel less threatened. 'Oh? From the sound of your voice, I take it that it wasn't exactly a raging success?' he said carefully.

'Nope,' she confirmed flatly. 'Boy meets girl. Girl gets bowled over. Boy promises her the world – so long as she's the one paying for it. Girl's father pays off boy. Boy leaves girl. Girl learns a big fat lesson. Think they could make a Hollywood movie out of it?' she asked, grinning determinedly across at him.

'Oh, bound too,' he said cheerfully. He was well aware that her joking manner was nothing but a front – a really good front, but one that didn't fool him for a minute. 'Who do you think would play you?' he mused. 'Julia Roberts?'

'Oh, at least Julia Roberts.'

'It must have hurt,' Gideon said simply, and she shot him a quick look. She shrugged.

'Oh, I got over it,' she said airily.

'After getting your self-confidence brutally battered,' he predicted softly. 'And after redefining what you wanted from life. And a few nights spent crying into your pillow. Not to mention an unwanted hardening of your shell, which has left you with a mistrust of men that you're scared will taint any of your future relationships. How am I doing?'

'Gee, Professor Welles, anyone would think you were a psychologist!'

'Cute.'

'Aren't I though?'

Gideon indicated left, knowing that they were not far from their destination and wishing he'd had more time to talk to her about all this.

He'd never really thought about Laurel Van Gilder as a vulnerable teenager before. As someone who'd taken hard knocks and come through. As someone, well, human, just like the rest of mankind.

One thing was for sure – he had no doubts that her run-in with a fortune hunter had left a very nasty scar indeed. Whether she was aware of it or not. And moreover, a scar of the worst kind. The kind you couldn't see.

But from now on, he was going to keep it very firmly in mind. For some reason that he wasn't yet ready to acknowledge, even to himself, he had the idea that one day – and perhaps soon – he was going to have to do something about that scar of hers.

Like heal it.

Forever.

He sighed heavily, then pulled the car over to the side of the road and parked. As he switched off the engine,

Laurel looked up at the small block of flats and then back to him. 'So, where are we?' she asked, shamelessly heading for safer ground and pushing the true confessions of the past few minutes firmly to the back of her mind.

Time enough to deal with them later.

'Dr Julie Ngabe's. She's got a house just around the corner.'

'You have been a busy little bee,' she mused getting out of the car, this time with a long-limbed easy grace.

Gideon watched her with hungry eyes, then got out himself. 'Oh, I've been even busier than that,' he said smugly.

'Oh?' she raised one black eyebrow in interrogation.

He locked the car and, as he moved to join her on the pavement, he held out his hand. He did it without really thinking about it. And, in the same manner, she took it. Suddenly, they found themselves on a cold and damp November afternoon, walking down a leaf-strewn pavement hand-in-hand.

'Er, yes,' Gideon said. Her hand felt so right in his. Not small, not delicate, not cold. It was a hand that he felt he could hold on to forever.

Laurel wondered if she should pull her hand free. But she didn't want to. Simple as that.

'What else have you found out then?' she asked instead, keeping her voice light and a little challenging.

Gideon responded to the overture thankfully. 'I've learned that Dr Ngabe's College, St Johns, has been reviewing her Research Fellowship.'

'Is that good or bad?'

Gideon launched into an explanation. 'A Research Fellowship is not a Full Fellowship. They can be anything from one year's duration to three or five. And they're renewable. Say a college wants to "check out" an academic. This academic has a good reputation and is doing some good work, but is still young and a relatively unknown factor. They offer him or her a Research Fellowship. That makes them an active member of the college – they get to teach and use the facilities, become an active force in the place.'

'But, at the end of the Fellowship, the college can get rid of them if they want,' Laurel followed him with ease.

'Right. But it's not all as bad as it sounds. Take one of your countrymen, for instance. He or she comes over here on a Rhodes Scholarship. Gets a good degree. Now, he's really got his eyes set on a full professorship at Yale, say. But the competition's tough. A three-year stint as an Oxford Fellow will give him a good CV and a massive boost up the ladder. Oxford gets a very able teacher with good credentials, who'll pull in other Rhodes Scholars and be a good contact afterwards. After three years, he goes off to Yale to commence battle and Oxford gets to snaffle up another Rhodes Scholar. Everyone wins.'

'Unless?' Laurel asked. For she was sure there was an 'unless' in that scenario somewhere.

'Unless what the Research Fellow really wants is to stay in Oxford full-time and hold a permanent post. Then the life of a Research Fellow gets to look pretty rocky.'

'But not if the college is happy with her,' Laurel pointed out.

'But what if it's not?'

Laurel glanced up at him. Being so tall, it was not often that she got the chance to look up at men. She found she rather liked it.

She liked the way the grey day around her couldn't diminish the silver-bright fairness of his hair. The way the grey mist had to give way to the power of his icy bright-blue eyes. She liked walking beside him. She liked the looks passers-by were giving them.

She forced herself to concentrate. 'Are you saying St Johns doesn't want to renew Julie Ngabe's Fellowship?'

'That's the word I heard. I have a friend at St Johns.'

I'll bet you do, she thought, with just a little pang of jealousy. For some reason, she was sure it was a female friend.

'I see. But I thought being shortlisted for the Van Gilder chair would have given her chances of renewal a boost.'

Gideon smiled. 'You don't know Oxford. What your Van Gilder panel might have thought impressive, doesn't apply here. There are enough toffee-nosed Dons who, secure in their own places, spend their time making life difficult for up-and comers.'

'Especially women?' Laurel said sourly.

'No. They're nasty to everyone. It's the old lion defending his territory against the young lion.'

'But surely St Johns must have some good Dons? They'd be cutting of their noses to spite their faces, if not.'

'I agree. And if Dr Ngabe had won the chair, then her tenure would have been assured, of that I have no doubt. But she didn't win. And I'm wondering just how bitter that might have made her, and what she might have done in the heat of the moment.'

'You mean steal the chalice?' Laurel said flatly.

Gideon sighed. 'It seems so far-fetched. But she might have seen taking the chalice as no more than her due. A sort of consolation prize.'

'Hmm. A nice psychological point of view,' Laurel mused. 'How about going for the more straightforward filthy money option. I don't suppose the good doctor has a big income?'

By now they'd reached the doctor's house. It was a modest semi, well-maintained, with a small, well-kept garden.

'Do you think she knows all this? About the college pulling the plug on her, I mean?' Laurel asked curiously.

Gideon shrugged. 'Why don't we ask her?'

'Yes.' Laurel sighed. 'Well, let's get on with it.'

Julie Ngabe opened the door herself. She was dressed in a bright orange and emerald green turban, with a matching flowing robe. She looked as beautiful, noble, and aloof as ever. Beside her, Laurel felt under-dressed and about as feminine as Oxtail soup.

'Professor Welles. How nice to see you again,' Dr Ngabe said graciously. 'And Miss Van Gilder. Please, do come in. I wasn't expecting visitors. Please excuse the state of the house.'

The house looked immaculate. Dusted, recently vacuumed, with not a dent in the cushions.

'Tea?'

'Please,' Gideon said, and allowed himself to be ushered into a living room and seated on a large, well-stuffed sofa. As their hostess went into the kitchen, Laurel and Gideon looked at each other helplessly.

'This is not going to be easy, is it?' Laurel said with massive understatement. And she was soon proved correct. Julie Ngabe returned with perfectly-made Indian tea and expensive wafer biscuits.

'I expect you're wondering what we're doing here,' Laurel blurted, a little unnerved by the other woman's quiet serenity.

Julie Ngabe smiled briefly and inclined her head.

'It's about the Augentine chalice,' Gideon took up the baton softly. 'We were wondering if you knew it had been stolen.'

For just a moment, the long, well-shaped hands hesitated as they raised the china teapot. Then Dr Ngabe calmly poured the first cup. 'No, this is the first I've heard of it. I haven't read the papers today.'

'I see. But it's not in the papers, Dr Ngabe. St Bedes is trying to…er…keep the situation under control. We were hoping to regain the chalice without any adverse publicity.'

Dr Ngabe looked at him steadily. 'That sounds very appropriate,' she said colourlessly. There was nothing in her voice that sounded like censure, but Gideon felt himself flushing.

Laurel sympathised with him. Dr Ngabe had a way of making you feel stupid, gauche, ugly, and ridiculous, without even trying. In fact, she was so cool, so in control, that it was not hard to imagine her as a competent thief.

One thing was for sure – if this woman had the chalice, there was no way she was going to give it back.

Laurel bit her lip, then bit into a biscuit and looked away.

'Did you notice anything odd at the party that night?' Gideon pressed on.

'Is that when the chalice was stolen?' Dr Ngabe allowed herself to sound surprised. 'Surely not. Not with so many people present. It was only out in the hall, wasn't it?'

Gideon nodded. 'Yes.'

'Then whoever took it took a great chance,' Dr Ngabe pointed out the obvious. 'Anyone could have left the party and caught the thief out.'

Gideon nodded. 'Yes. It was an act of desperation, all right. Or perhaps anger?'

Dr Ngabe's eyes flickered. Then she inclined her head

graciously. 'Or, as you say, an act of anger.'

'Were you surprised that I won the chair, Dr Ngabe?' Gideon asked. He felt awkward questioning this proud, aloof woman. Like it was he who had done something wrong.

Dr Ngabe stiffened, visibly. But was that just embarrassment? Gideon wondered.

'No. Of all of us, you were the strongest candidate. Of course, in a few years time…' she shrugged delicately, but the message was clear.

Dr Ngabe didn't see herself as anybody's 'also-ran'.

Gideon nodded. 'Yes. I agree. So, to get back to the theft. Did you notice anybody leave the party for any length of time?'

'You did,' Dr Ngabe said – and was there just a hint of a smile on her inscrutable, ebony face?

Gideon inclined his head. 'Yes. Anyone else?'

'We are concentrating on those of us who overheard your Dean announce some sort of problem with the alarm, I take it?' she said calmly and sipped her tea.

Laurel felt herself watching her in open admiration. Was this some class act or what?

'Yes, we are,' Gideon admitted. 'For obvious reasons.'

Dr Ngabe seemed to think. She was quiet – and utterly still – for about the space of five seconds. 'Sir Laurence never left the room at all. Dr Doyle did so, but only for a few minutes. Dr Ollenbach was gone the longest, I think.'

'And yourself?' It was Laurel who put the question in. She managed, somehow, not to make it sound too impertinent.

'No. Like Sir Laurence, I never left the room – except to leave it to go home, of course,' she added.

Laurel glanced at Gideon. Now there was a thought.

Had the thief simply nicked the chalice on the way out?

But no. Surely not. That would just be too suicidal. The later the hour, the more likely it would be that someone else would also be leaving the party and catch the thief red-handed.

So was she just blowing smoke? Laurel wouldn't put it past her. Anyone who could be quite so sphinx-like bore careful consideration.

Gideon, however, was less inclined to read anything sinister in the doctor's flat tone. He knew that to a woman of Dr Ngabe's refinement, maintaining a polite and deferential veneer at all times was a top priority.

'You did your first Ph.D. in Nairobi, I believe?' he changed tack abruptly. If she seemed surprised, it didn't show.

'Yes.'

'And you're now working on a D.Phil.,' Gideon said conversationally. 'I look forward to reading your thesis once it's published.'

'Thank you.'

'I mean it,' Gideon said softly. 'I think it will be well worth reading.'

Her calm brown eyes met his. He couldn't tell if she was angry at him – suspecting that he was just being patronising – or whether she found praise from a man of his standing genuinely satisfying.

He sighed. No doubt about it. If this woman was responsible for the theft, she was not about to give herself away. Still. He couldn't just give up.

'Your Research Fellowship runs until the end of next Trinity term doesn't it, Dr Ngabe?' he asked casually.

'It does.'

'I hope, at the end of it, you might apply to St Bedes for another post. I'm sure Lord St John James wouldn't be averse to adding another psychologist to the college prospectus.'

It was a clever ploy, Laurel realised at once. If Dr Ngabe jumped at it, then they would know that she knew that St Johns was going to kick her out.

Dr. Ngabe smiled politely. 'That's very flattering, Professor Welles,' she said politely.

And that, thought Laurel wryly, was an even cleverer ploy. It gave absolutely nothing away.

Gideon, too, knew when he was hitting his head against a brick wall. He finished his tea, made professional psychological small talk for a while, and then rose to excuse himself.

Laurel took his hint and the good doctor showed them to the door. On the way back to the car, Laurel felt a depressing sense of *déjà vu*.

'We've gone this route before,' she mused glumly.

'I know. And how much further forward are we?' he agreed. They climbed in the car and he turned the engine. 'Where to now?'

'Why not go back to your place?' she asked. 'Put our heads together and see what we come up with? Then we can track down the Don who was taking photographs that night. Although what good pictures will do us, I can't say. Unless you can use some secret psycho-powers and point out the guilty one just by looking at his or her picture?'

'I'm not Clark Kent,' Gideon said wryly.

As they got into the car, Gideon, for the first time ever, felt reluctant to head for St Bedes. He fought the sensation off and drove swiftly back to the Woodstock Road.

Walking through the quads, past the War Memorial and through Becket Arch, they both noticed that the college had a curiously breathless air about it. As if the very buildings were waiting for something to happen.

The last time she'd been in this room, Laurel thought as Gideon ushered her into his spacious quarters and closed the door behind them, she'd just discovered that the chalice was missing. She'd been in shock and seeking refuge.

Now it was nearly four o'clock and already getting dark.

She watched Gideon walk to the windows and draw across the long velvet curtains. He moved confidently around in the dark, turning on lamps, and then walked to the drink's cabinet. 'Brandy?'

'Please.'

Laurel sank down on the sofa. Gideon handed her a drink, then walked over to the grate. A scout had laid out a log fire all ready to light. Although the radiators had kept the chill off the room, she was glad to see a cheery flame flicker amongst the coal and paper. Soon there was a blaze going. That and the brandy warmed her through. Funny, she hadn't realised how cold she'd been until then.

Wearily, Gideon stretched out on the white sheepskin rug in front of the fire. He often lay there, but to Laurel, who'd been expecting him to draw up a chair, or better yet sit next to her on the sofa, the manoeuvre came as a complete surprise.

She watched him lie out, like a long, lean polar bear, and noticed how the firelight played such wonderful, loving tricks with the colour of his hair and eyes, and on the planes of his cheeks.

Looking into the flames, Gideon sighed. 'Well, let's recap. The Ollenbachs definitely seem to value money, and might be in financial straits. And there's certainly tension between husband and wife. I think she's quite desperate to keep him happy – and I think he's a very expensive possession.'

'Agreed,' Laurel said. Her eyes were still on his profile.

Sitting so close to the fire made Gideon take off his sweater. The wool teased his fine fair hair, leaving it as wispy as cobwebs where the static electricity had made it dance.

He leaned back on his elbows, his long legs stretched out towards the door.

'Dr Ngabe, on the other hand, is another definite contender. She needed to win the chair in order to keep her Oxford place and when she knew she wasn't going to get it – who knows? Also, if she was desperate enough to stay on here, she might have been inclined to secure for herself a fair whack of money, if only in the hopes of going independent and financing her own research.'

'And she's got the temperament for it,' Laurel put in. 'She'd be good at whatever she tried to do. Level-headed. Calm. In control.'

Gideon sighed. 'But has she got the right psychological make-up to take such a chance? I just can't see Dr Ngabe taking such a risk. If caught, she'd have gone to jail. She'd certainly have lost all chance of a life in Oxford. I just can't see her risking it. Her personality is all wrong for that.'

'And let's not forget your precious Dr Doyle,' Laurel said waspishly. 'Keeping your face and figure at her age costs a lot of money.'

Gideon glanced across at her, surprised by the venom in her voice.

'Martha? Martha's been in Oxford for years. Longer than I have. She's got a good solid background. She wrote a blinder of a D.Phil. thesis and has been a member of one of the city's oldest colleges for years. She seems secure enough. Besides, I've never heard of her needing money. She hasn't got any expensive hidden vices that I know about.'

And you'd know, wouldn't you? Laurel thought waspishly, her lips twisting. 'A bit protective of her, aren't you?' she mocked.

Gideon frowned. 'Martha? No, not particularly. Why?'

Laurel flushed. 'Nothing,' she muttered.

Gideon turned on one elbow, the better to look at her. An odd expression suddenly crossed his face. Half-smile, half-disbelief.

'You're jealous!' he said incredulously.

'I am not!' Laurel flared, slamming down her brandy glass and falling to her knees beside him. 'I just found it sickening, watching her flirt with you in a public place, that's all. Restaurants are for eating food. Not undressing men with your eyes,' she snorted primly.

Gideon laughed. 'Oh that! Martha's a born flirt. She does it with all men.'

'Shut up!' Laurel growled. His laughter was doing odd things to her insides. He had such white strong teeth. Such a deep-timbered laugh, it seemed to roll and echo through the walls of her stomach.

Suddenly all laughter fled. Gideon looked at her, saw her eyes darken, and shook his head. 'Laurel, no,' he said, but his voice had lost all its power.

She pushed him back on to the rug, moving over him.

'I thought we agreed,' he began weakly.

'So I lied,' she said huskily. And kissed him. Her hands moved between them, seeking the buttons of his shirt and ripping them apart. His flesh felt warm from the fire, but now it began to burn with a different heat altogether.

Her lips left his. He breathed out tremulously.

'Laurel.'

She dipped her mouth to the indentation between his throat and neck and kissed and licked there. He swallowed hard, his eyes feathering closed. 'Laurel,' he said again. A moan. A wonderment.

She pushed the flaps of his shirt off his shoulders, revealing a long, deep chest, scattered with fine silvery hairs. Her fingers ran across his skin, caressing and pinching, and she growled in response to the way he twitched to her touch, like a man being electrocuted.

Her mouth moved along the fine contours of his shoulders, to nibble on his earlobe, before moving down his rib cage, lower, lower, until her tongue burrowed into his navel.

Gideon moaned, his legs jerking in spasms of response.

'Please,' he said. But by now he had no idea what he was pleading for.

Laurel moved her hand against the bulge in his jeans and pressed hard. She could feel him move beneath her, harden and throb like an animal stirred from hibernation.

Gideon groaned, a long, drawn-out moan of near-pain. Feverishly, she dealt with his belt buckle and zip. Before he could even gather together a scattered thought, she pulled off his boots and stripped him naked, yanking off his jeans as if she hated them.

She kissed his kneecap.

Gideon gasped. This wasn't possible. Since when was a kneecap an erogenous zone? Then she moved up his thigh, kissing and nibbling his jumping tendons and he realised that with this woman, his whole body was an erogenous zone.

And it was time to find out if the same held true with her!

Laurel yelped in surprise as she suddenly found herself

flat on her back, his silver head looming over her. His mouth on hers was a marauder, chasing out her tongue, battling it, winning, always winning.

She felt her own clothes melting away, felt his hands on her flesh, long-fingered, sensitive and…

She sighed. A long, drawn-out breath of pleasure as he placed his palms over her breasts and slowly, gently, squeezed. Through a daze, she saw his silver head lower, then felt the hot, moist, thrusting touch of his tongue around her nipple.

She growled. And suddenly moved her legs apart, lifting and hooking them around the small of his back.

Gideon grunted in surprise. For a long second, he resisted the pressure of her strong limbs. Then his body lowered to hers, joined hers, fitting them together like two pieces of a jigsaw puzzle.

Laurel's eyes widened as she felt him enter her. He filled her, stretched and caressed her, demanding and yet delivering. She felt her internal muscles clench around him. Above her, she saw his eyes widen. Dazzle. Soften.

'Laurel,' he said. Firm. Sure. Contented.

Laurel watched his face contort as they began to dance together. Her legs tightened on him, her heels digging into his buttocks, allowing him no chance of escape.

All trace of the tall, cold, imperious man disappeared. In his place was her lover. His brow beading with sweat, his icy-blue eyes softening into pools of molten desire. His lean jaw fell open as he breathed in great gasping gulps of air.

And she knew her own face must bear the same intense concentration of sensation and desire.

Love and lust.

Greed and generosity.

She felt her body spiralling out of control. She felt her

own sweat-damp hair fly around her face as she thrashed her head from side-to-side.

'Gideon!' she wailed, bucking under him, the tendons in her neck straining as she arched her back and her fingernails raked across his back.

Gideon screamed. There was no other word for the sound he made as he felt his body melt and flow into the hot waiting pool of her womanhood.

He collapsed against her, the echo of her own scream ringing in his ears.

Laurel raised her hands to accept him as he fell against her. Her fingers tenderly brushed away the hair from his temples.

Her own breast rose and fell heavily. His head, resting against her, moved up and down in time to her breathing.

Melting the iceman had been wonderful.

chapter eleven

'Is this the place?' Laurel asked, slipping off her seat-belt and looking at the tiny but charming little terraced cottage in front of her.

'It is,' Gideon agreed, getting out and coming around to open her door for her. As she alighted, his eyes fell to her legs, noting the dimple in her knees.

He didn't look away.

Laurel straightened, catching the name of the street. 'Magpie Lane. Cute names you British give things. Were there magpies here once?' she asked, turning to him, catching him quickly looking up.

Gideon smiled and shrugged. 'I don't know. Ask a historian. If you've got six hours to spare.'

Laurel held out her hands in a gesture of defeat. 'No way. I'm getting used to the way your cronies work. I ask if there were magpies here once, and I'll probably get told of a legendary story to do with some king eight hundred years ago. Or a terrible baker who did awful things with birds back in 1602. And it was all to do with social economic atrocities committed by a rebel government who…' She went on to do a great imitation of a British drone, capable of going on and on for hours. 'No thanks!' she laughed.

They had come to the home of the Don who'd been taking pictures of the party on the fateful night.

'This guy's not an historian, is he?' Laurel whispered nervously, as they walked up the path and she watched as Gideon lifted the highly-polished brass door knocker and rapped it twice. 'No. Worse. He's an economist. Whatever you do, don't mention Dennis Healey.'

Laurel blinked. 'Who's Dennis…ooh!'

The last because the door was opening, and she'd suddenly discovered Gideon's bony elbow digging into her ribs.

'Hello George.'

'Gideon!'

The man in front of them was just how Laurel remembered him from the party – small, neat and dapper, with a cap of rather oily-looking black hair and a wayward moustache. He was dressed in an Argyle sweater and jeans.

Laurel blinked.

'This is a surprise. And Miss Van Gilder too. Thank you for bringing her to see me, Gideon. Well, do come in, come in, come in.'

Somewhat gingerly they entered the tiny cottage, and were shown to a neat little sitting room. Their host quickly returned from the kitchen with a tray of tea and crumpets.

Gideon glanced at the clock. It was nearly four.

Laurel shook her head. It really was true – everything stopped for tea in this country.

Or at least, it did in Oxford.

Or in Oxford Dons' houses.

'So, how are you enjoying our city of dreaming spires, m'dear?' the little man asked and Laurel, realising with a start that he was talking to her, swallowed her tea (and a desire to tell him she wasn't anyone's 'dear') and smiled.

'Fine. I was wondering, er…'

'George Fairbairn, m'dear. Everyone calls me George. Except my wife – she calls me Georgie.'

Laurel bit her lip – hard – and avoided Gideon's eye. 'Er, George. I was wondering if you'd had the pictures you took at the party developed yet,' she plunged right in. After Gideon's warning, she could imagine them being stuck here for hours, gossiping about anything and nothing.

Georgie looked the type.

'She means at the Van Gilder prize-giving in St Bedes,' Gideon said helpfully as George looked puzzled.

'Oh – those. Yes, of course. I've got them somewhere, now where did I put them? Oh, of course. Just a moment.'

He shot off the chair and went out into the hall, and Gideon leaned closer to Laurel. 'George is a serial socialiser. He's probably been to ten other parties since ours. And I'm not exaggerating!'

'Good on Georgie,' Laurel hissed back, and Gideon only just succeeding in hiding his grin as George returned with a big pack of photos.

'Here they are. They came out quite well, even if I have to blow my own trumpet. I was trying out a new flash system.'

And before they could reign him in, he was off.

Both his visitors let his stream of explanation wash over them as they examined the photographs.

Laurel, of course, looked exquisite, just as Gideon remembered. But it soon become clear George had reason to boast of his prowess because the photos were excellent. Sin-Jun, Rex, all their suspects, as well as strangers to them both, had been caught on film for all eternity, perfectly-lighted and candid.

But in not one of them was the door to the Senior common room open, giving an illicit glimpse of someone outside stealing the chalice.

Of course, neither had expected that. Miracles might

have been attributed to the chalice in the past, but neither of them had been expecting divine intervention during this particular quest. Still, it would have been nice if the photos had given just a hint of help.

'Dr Ngabe looks almost regal in this one,' Gideon murmured, handing over a picture of the African woman in her bright tribal robe.

'Your Martha looks a little worse for drink in this one,' Laurel couldn't help but point out with a twinge of satisfaction, as she handed a photo of her own over.

'I wish you wouldn't keep harping on about her,' Gideon said back, then glanced up as he'd realised George had finally stopped speaking.

'Looking for anything nice in particular?' the little man asked brightly, his bird-keen eyes looking from one to the other speculatively.

Gideon flushed, almost guessing what he was thinking. Only lovers carped on like they'd been doing.

Well, they were lovers!

He smiled at the thought, then noticed that George was waiting for a reply and floundered.

'Yes,' Laurel, sensing his unease, leapt into the breech. 'We were hoping to find one of us together. To commemorate the first night we met.'

George beamed. Obviously he was on to something here. Romances were always his favourite form of gossip. (Politics and economics, of course, were, in George's book, far too serious a subject to ever be classed as mere chit-chat!)

'Let me see. I think, yes, here's one,' he said, relieving Gideon of half his pile and pulling one out.

George had caught them perfectly, Gideon realised at once, during their brief argument.

He was glowering down at her and she was glaring

up at him.

'Er, an interesting composition,' George said tactfully. Anything less lovey-dovey was hard to imagine.

Laurel, however, swooped. 'Perfect,' she said with a mischievous grin. 'I think it captures the mood of the moment just right. Don't you, darling?'

Gideon's eyes widened as he shot her a killing look.

'If you say so. Sweetheart,' he gritted back. And glanced, resignedly, at George. Come tomorrow it would be all over town that he and Laurel were an item.

Strangely, though, the thought didn't dismay him as much as he'd thought it might.

'Oh, here's one of Dr Ollenbach. A nice piece, isn't it?' George said. Then, aware of two pairs of eyes looking at him incredulously, he blurted out, 'The pendant, I mean. A real diamond. I'm a bit of a jewellery buff, you see. My dear lady wife does so like gems.'

And he sighed. Rather unhappily, Laurel felt, and hid yet another grin.

She took the picture off George and looked at it. He was right – the pendant was small but, even in a photograph, she could tell that the diamond drop was real.

Absently, she passed the photograph over.

And Gideon froze.

He stared down at the photograph for a long time, until first Laurel and then George noticed his preoccupation.

'What is it?' Laurel asked softly.

Gideon started, then shook his head. 'Oh. Er, nothing. Look George, it was really good of you to let us have a look through the pictures. Are you sure you don't mind us having this one,' he asked, nodding to the photograph Laurel clutched possessively in her hand and getting up.

'No, of course not. Going so soon?' he asked, obviously disappointed.

'Yes. We have an appointment. With the Principal,' he added firmly as George was obviously about to demur.

'Oh yes, I see,' he muttered at once. Interviews with Principals were obviously not something to be trifled with, Laurel thought with a pang of tenderness.

No doubt about it, Oxford – and its academic way of life – was beginning to find a place in her affections.

Containing her impatience only with the greatest of effort, she followed Gideon out and then hopped frustrated from foot-to-foot as George kept them talking on the doorstep.

Eventually they got away and, at the gate, Laurel could stand it no longer.

'What?' she demanded. 'What?'

'In the car,' Gideon said, looking around at the passing pedestrians nervously. 'I've been an idiot. A first-class dolt.'

Laurel snorted. Now that she couldn't believe.

'OK, so what have you been an idiot about,' she demanded once they'd buckled up and Gideon had turned the engine on. The low throaty purr of the Morgan gave them an obliging amount of privacy as Gideon leaned towards her.

'What was the first thing we established about the theft of the chalice?' he asked annoyingly.

Why did men find it so hard to come to the point? she wondered mutinously.

'That it must have been one of the shortlisted candidates who pinched it,' she hazarded impatiently.

Gideon jerked his hand angrily in the air. 'Yes, but apart from that?' And when she continued to looked puzzled and irked, he prompted, 'that it had to be a spur of the moment thing, right?'

'Right.'

'So, if it was spur of the moment…how did the thief manage to cut a hole in the glass? Do you usually go to parties with a burglary gadget in your handbag?' he demanded.

'No. So what…' Suddenly her eyes widened. 'Diamonds cut glass,' she said, catching on instantly.

'Right. Dr Ngabe was wearing beads, I noticed from the photos. I hadn't got a diamond on me, and Martha's not a big fan either. If she was wearing jewellery, I'd bet it was gold or silver.'

'And you'd know her tastes, of course.'

'Laurel! Damn it woman, keep your mind focused. Don't you get it? Now we know who did it.'

Laurel nodded slowly. She leaned back in her chair and sighed. 'I wish it hadn't been the fellow American,' she said, somewhat irrelevantly.

Gideon shook his head. 'They have to be in deep financial trouble for her to do something so desperate. I wonder if a hundred grand will even be enough.'

'I doubt they'd get that. Even from a good fence,' Laurel said then broke off, an appalled look on her face. She suddenly reached up and smacked the palm of her hand against her forehead. 'What a twit I am. You talk about you being dim!'

'What?'

'A fence. Can you see either Dr Ollenbach or that husband of hers even knowing a fence?' she challenged.

'No,' Gideon said promptly. Then his eyes widened. 'So how are they going to sell it?'

Laurel grinned. 'Only one way, buddy boy. Only one way.'

In their house on Five Mile Drive, Dr Felicity Ollenbach sat in her chair and stared at the Augentine chalice. Her husband, still reeling from the shock, sat beside her. Numbly he pointed at the small silver receptacle.

'And you're telling me that that's really worth over a hundred grand?' he asked, his voice suitably awed.

'Yes,' Felicity said flatly.

She stared at the chalice in almost the same disbelief as her husband.

Even after all these days, she could still hardly believe she'd stolen it. She just couldn't believe what had come over her.

That night she'd been totally on edge, right from the beginning. Even though winning the Van Gilder chair wouldn't have been enough to keep them solvent for long, it would have given them breathing space.

And the promise of added income.

On the strength of winning it, she might even have managed to get another book accepted with a sizeable advance.

Her stomach had been tied in knots as she'd sat down to dinner in St Bedes Hall. It had been impossible to eat a thing. Indeed, she'd even had to force herself to keep from staring at Laurel Van Gilder like a child in a sweet shop, so badly did she need the woman to announce her own name.

When Laurel had stood up to deliver her speech and present the chair, she'd clenched her fists and wished, wished so hard, like a child making a wish when watching a falling star, that the Van Gilder woman would say her name.

But she had spoken the name of Gideon Welles instead. Gideon, a bachelor, living in college, with no need of added income, no attachments – a man with nothing to lose.

It had been so unfair.

Still was so unfair.

And then to have to go to the party afterwards. To smile and talk and pretend losing hadn't meant anything. The resentment had seethed inside her, boiling, like slow-acting poison.

When she'd walked into the Senior common room hall behind Gideon, that military-looking Principal of theirs and Laurel Van Gilder, and heard the Dean say that the alarm on the cabinet wasn't working, she hadn't even given it a thought.

Not then.

It had only been later – after several brandies, that she'd remembered about the alarm being faulty.

Even then, the thought of thievery hadn't occured to her. She'd been too steeped in self-pity. And fear. She'd drunk some more and contemplated her debts. The thought of not being able to meet the next mortgage repayment. Or the next. The ever-looming horror of losing Brian.

And the more she'd thought, the more she'd fingered her diamond pendant. It had long since been her nervous habit to finger whatever piece of jewellery she was wearing – twisting a ring around and around her finger. Unclasping and clasping a watchband. But she'd carelessly hurt her fingers by holding on too tight to the diamond, which had led to a semi-drunken thought about how hard a diamond was – the hardest substance of all. How it could even cut glass.

And right then and there it had occured to her. It was almost laughable.

Some Sociology Don was going on about something or other. Two men were laughing smugly in a corner. The College Butler was circulating sedately with drinks. It was Oxford at its most established.

And she'd stood amidst it all, and realised that she had the wherewithal to steal the chalice. It had felt absurd. But right. So curiously, funnily, right.

The alarm wasn't working.

She could cut a round hole in the glass with her diamond.

Reach in, take the chalice. Take it home. Sell it. All her problems would be solved – for a while.

And so she'd done it.

Just like that.

She'd been drunk, of course. Eaten alive with disappointment, rage and bravado, she'd half-expected to be caught. Imagined her defiance in the face of it. But in the event, the door to the Senior common room simply hadn't opened!

It had been easier than she'd thought to cut the hole and push the cut piece of glass into the cabinet – it hadn't even broken but had clattered on to one of the shelves whole. It had taken only seconds to reach in, lift the small silver cup, and slip it into her handbag.

Then she'd noticed the Butler's big black coat hanging on a hook and, in a moment of inspiration, draped it across the cabinet, hiding her work.

Then she'd driven home – very carefully and slowly. She shouldn't have been driving.

Funny, but when she thought back to that night, the drink-driving shamed her more than the theft.

After all, what did it matter to a family as fabulously wealthy as the Van Gilders if she relieved them of one of their little treasures?

And St Bedes didn't need it.

But she did.

Dammit, she did. It was almost the difference between life and death to her. So why shouldn't she have it?

It made more sense.

But afterwards. Ah, afterwards, things had looked different. Very different indeed.

Oh, not that night. She'd driven back to the party, chatted and circulated, and then finally left with a group of others, all in a state of numbness. But the next morning, however, had brought with it a hangover and stark reality.

She'd been mad! Mad! To think she could get away with it for a start. She'd spent all the day on tenterhooks, expecting any minute to have a call from the police. To be carted off in handcuffs, to face shame and, worst of all, a visit from Brian telling her that he was leaving her.

For she had no illusions about her husband. He would not stay with her if she ever became a liability.

He needed a stable home, the little luxuries he so enjoyed, the status of having an Oxford Don for a wife. All those things mattered to him as he sought his own fame and fortune on the stage.

Perhaps, in the back of his mind, he doubted himself and his luck, and wondered if he'd ever make it. Which made having a rich wife even more of an imperative.

She'd hidden the chalice in the washing machine wrapped in a sweater, secure in the knowledge that it would remain hidden – from Brian, at least. He didn't even know how the washing machine worked.

But no police had come.

Only Gideon Welles (of all people!) and Laurel Van Gilder herself.

Brian had been angry by their visit, by all their questions. He'd been (ridiculous to think of it now) genuinely indignant on her behalf at their insinuations. He hadn't even asked her if she'd stolen the chalice. He simply couldn't imagine her having the nerve or the gumption to take it, she realised now.

Just goes to show how little he knew her.

So when, just a few minutes ago, she'd finally confessed the truth to him and produced the chalice as proof, he'd looked so incredibly surprised.

Now husband and wife sat and stared at the Augentine chalice. Finally, Brian reached out and touched it, almost reluctantly, and lifted it up, weighing it up and down in his hand.

'It's heavy.'

'Yes,' Felicity said listlessly. 'Brian, what are we going to do? Do you think Laurel Van Gilder meant it – about not calling in the police? That was the unspoken promise, wasn't it – that if they got it back, there'd be no scandal. No mention of it even having been missing?'

'Give it back? Are you mad? It's worth over a hundred grand, Flick. Think of it. A hundred thousand quid.'

His handsome face flushed with pleasure as he stared down at the silver object in his hand.

Felicity sighed. 'I was mad to take it.'

'Course you weren't. Why should they have all the luck?' Brian instantly went on the defensive. 'Look, you can't really think we can just hand this back and they won't do nothing about it do you?' he wheedled. 'Besides, why should we? You risked everything for this – we might as well make the most of it.'

In his mind's eye, he could see himself driving a new Porsche. A wardrobe from Armani. Or producing his own play, casting himself in the lead of course. Yes, that was it. If it was successful, they'd make more than the chalice was worth in the first run.

Felicity sighed. 'Brian, darling, come down to planet

earth for a moment. How on earth are we supposed to sell it?'

She'd been too drunk, and too angry, the night she'd taken it to even consider the practicalities.

'Do you know someone who receives stolen goods?' Felicity asked, half-hopefully, half-mockingly. Brian was a dreamer and practically useless.

But her husband, occasionally, surprised her.

He surprised her now.

'Don't be daft, Flick. It's no use going to one of those sort. What we need is a collector. Someone who won't care how or where a piece comes from. He'll give us top money for it and guarantee that no cops will ever become involved. Now, let's get on the Internet. There's bound to be some old codger on there who'd be only to glad to add something like this,' and he waggled the antique silver relic at her 'to his mouldy old collection.'

'If you want to know about a collector of sixteenth-century silver, ask a Don,' Gideon said as he turned into the gates of St Bedes.

On the way back from George's, Laurel had told him what had suddenly occurred to her. Namely – that the Ollenbachs, if they had any sense at all, would try and sell the chalice to a collector rather than a fence. It would be easier, safer, and they'd get better money.

'Fine. Which Don?' she asked, clambering out after him.

'Any Don,' Gideon said grimly. 'Rex would know about clerical silver. A Classics Don would know someone in a museum who knows someone. Get the idea?'

'Right. How about someone in your Fine Art department?'

In the event, Gideon preferred going to someone he knew – Rex – and found him easily enough in the chapel.

He was snoozing in one of the pews, a theology paper from one of his pupils scattered around him and the latest Cantata from the choir-master awaiting his perusal, slipping from his lap on to the floor.

He started awake at the sound of their entrance and was quick to help when Gideon, without any preamble, asked him if he knew who the biggest collector of silver in town was.

'Oh, Francis Daye, without doubt,' the cleric said, sitting up straight and rubbing his eyes. 'Made a fortune in the booming eighties and had the sense to get out in time. Now he does nothing but collect Celtic artefacts and old silver. And cats, I believe. He lives out near Chipping Norton way, in one of those tiny hamlets – Dene, I think it is. Why?'

But Gideon and Laurel were interestingly evasive and quickly dismissed themselves.

Rex watched them go, somewhat bemused.

'We have to find Sin-Jun,' Gideon said the moment they'd shut the big oak chapel door behind them. 'He'll have the necessary clout to tackle the Ollenbachs or this Francis Daye, if they've already sold the chalice on.'

'Right,' Laurel said.

But Sin-Jun, for once, was nowhere to be found. His secretary, to make matters even worse, had obviously already gone home for the day.

'He'll be back for dinner,' Gideon said. 'Let's wait in my room.'

Laurel, however, soon discovered she didn't have the patience for waiting. After five minutes of pacing his room like a caged tiger, she needed something to distract her.

She looked at Gideon, who was sat lounging in his big armchair, looking perfectly relaxed. Until she noticed the book in his hands was upside down.

She advanced on him, smiling wolfishly.

'Here's one. That's the name of a village near here, isn't it?' Felicity said, staring at the computer screen over her husband's shoulder. 'It says here – he's interested in all manner of old silver.'

'Yeah. He sounds like a contender all right. He lives in an out-of-the-way place – made his money in property – that's a crook's domain if ever there was one,' Brian said gleefully. 'Francis Daye. I reckon he might be just what the doctor ordered. I'll phone and sound him out.'

Gideon moaned.

His bare feet were dangling over the bed, since no standard-made bed ever fitted him. He was naked, his arms spread-eagled across the pillows, and Laurel was sucking so hard on his navel he was sure she was about to suck it right out of him.

The ceiling above him seemed to be turning in a slow, crazy circle.

'I was so proud of you when you came up with that "diamond cutting glass" business,' she mumbled, her mouth full of his hot, pulsating flesh. 'You're quite a Sherlock Holmes, aren't you?'

She lifted her head and ran her hands lightly down his chest. She watched the sensitive nerve-endings in his stomach twitch and jump, and dipped her head to kiss them.

Gideon moaned again.

'I was just as impressed with your collector theory,' he gasped, his voice coming out with all the calmness of an out-of-control see-saw.

He closed his eyes briefly but that only made the sensations a thousand times more potent.

He moaned again.

Laurel smiled. She liked that sound he made. She wanted to go right on listening to it for the rest of her life.

Abruptly, too needy to go on playing with him, she lowered herself on to him, making a sound all of her own. A kind of purring rumble.

Gideon arched his back compulsively, but she wouldn't be dislodged. He felt her thighs tighten around his own, felt her feminine muscles tighten seductively around him, and his hands clenched into compulsive fists either side of his head.

He felt his body become slick with sweat. A tight, spiralling core of intense and ruthless pleasure began to build in his loins.

Laurel moved rhythmically on top of him, slowly, sensuously, her face tense with concentration and greedy expectation.

She'd never been so completely herself with a man before. Always before, she'd been playing a role. The rich heiress sorting out her suitors. The playful playgirl, going to the right parties and giving the paparazzi the right pictures of the right man on her arm.

Never before had she felt free to just be herself. Whether it was bailing him out of a jam, just talking to him in his low-slung car, or making love to him in a bed that didn't quite fit!

'Oh Gideon, I love you so much.'

It wasn't until he suddenly stilled beneath her that she realised she'd spoken the thought out loud.

Her eyes snapped open. She looked down at him, only to find his ice-blue eyes staring up at her.

He looked so startled, she had to laugh.

'Don't worry,' she said softly. 'I won't hold it against you.'

She fought back a lance of fear at her own stupidity in not being able to keep her big mouth shut for once, and leaned back, placing her hands on his shins and clenching herself around him. Time to distract him, before he got the chance to become thoroughly spooked!

He moaned again as the spiralling tension became almost a pain. Laurel, too, began to move faster, harder, deeper, her long black hair rippling around her shoulders, falling to brush his legs as she threw her head back, her throat taut with passion.

His eyes narrowed into languorous desire as he looked at her, her pert, cherry-tipped breasts peaking between swathes of her raven-black hair, her face abandoned, her cheekbones impossibly sharp, her eyes closed, her mouth slightly parted.

She was so magnificent that he felt himself unravelling. His body was her puppet. She'd turned his head around. She'd pulled his life inside out.

And he didn't care.

She loved him!

She'd said so.

He moaned again. The moan turning into a low shout of released desire as he melted into liquid fire and poured himself into her.

Laurel shuddered and slowly collapsed on to him, her long black hair falling around them as they slept the sleep of the exhausted.

Laurel's sole cookery skill consisted of toasting bread and squeezing oranges, and it was these two smells that roused him a while later.

He must have dozed, for he couldn't remember her leaving his bed.

He showered (having to duck in the standard-sized shower stall), and found her in the kitchen, reading the evening papers and avoiding his eyes.

Gideon set about the ultra-British pastime of making tea, watched her drink her own coffee, and wondered if he should talk about what she'd said just now.

It seemed to loom there – all important, undeniable – like a huge brick wall.

'So, do you have any idea what to try next?' Laurel said, bright and breezily, as she lowered the newspaper and looked at him, her eyes dark as plain chocolate. 'If Sin-Jun has gone for the weekend or something, I mean?'

He blinked. 'About what, exactly?' he asked cautiously.

'About getting the chalice back of course,' Laurel said, fighting back a nervous laugh. At all costs, she had to make what had just happened seem like no big deal.

Like she said 'I love you' all the time.

'We can't just sit here and do nothing. Not now we know who might have the chalice.'

'Laurel.'

'We could always confront the Ollenbachs. If it's still at their home, we can bring in back in triumph,' she gabbled desperately. 'Can't you just see Sin-Jun's face, walking into the Senior common room and there the chalice is, right back where it started?'

She looked so on edge, so taut and on the verge of tears, that he felt like reaching out and…

'I love you too,' he said helplessly.

chapter twelve

'You what?' Laurel screeched, her whole face lighting up like a nuclear explosion and Gideon took a hasty step backwards.

'Wait a moment, woman,' he warned but she was already launching herself at him.

Luckily, he caught her.

The next moment, his face was being smothered with tiny kisses – his nose, his eyes, eyebrows, lips, cheeks, chin, forehead. And he was grinning like an idiot.

Her legs were hooked around his waist, and he walked with her into the centre of the room, heading towards the sofa.

'Will you please just wait a minute, wait a minute,' he muffled through her hair, her lips, her hands.

'Wait for what?' Laurel demanded, laughing and lifting her head. Cradled against him as she was, held high on his chest, she was looking down into his eyes for the first time. They really were the colour of ice – a pale electric-blue fire.

She brushed the near-white hair off his forehead and sighed happily. 'Gideon, I'm so happy,' she said simply.

'Well, I never would have guessed,' he said drolly.

'Don't grouch. You know full well you're happy too.'

And he was.

His heart was thudding, while at the same time soaring. He shook his head. 'Are you going to let go of me now?' he demanded, but couldn't seem to get any force into his voice.

Laurel looked over and down her shoulders, to where his arms were locked around the small of her back.

Gideon, in response, did the same, to where her heels pressed hard into his buttocks.

'You started it,' he said softly.

Laurel sighed and unlocked her legs, and he slithered her carefully down his body, groaning slightly as he did so.

'Was that a moan I heard?' she asked archly.

'No!' he said quickly. As she moved to come back into his arms, he pressed one hand flat against her chest – and instantly became aware of her burgeoning nipple pressing against his index finger.

'Stay there,' he said sternly and dropped his hand.

'Yes master.'

'We've got to talk.'

'Whatever you say, Oh Great One.'

'Cut it out. Humility, even the mock variety, doesn't suit you. We've got to discuss what we're going to do?'

'About the chalice?'

'No, you great American ninny. About us.'

'What about us?' Laurel asked, arching a brow, lost in the giddy state of being both euphoric and dead scared at the same time. For what would come now?

'You said you love me,' Gideon said, his voice quiet and serious. 'Is that true or was it just, you know, in the heat of the moment?'

Laurel's smile slowly faded. This was no time for fun.

'It was true. It started the night the chalice got stolen and I came to your room. Or maybe even before that. When you visited me in hospital.'

'I was rotten to you when I visited you in hospital,' he pointed out.

'True. But what's that got to do with anything? Do you love me? Or did you just say that in a fit of madness?'

Gideon shook his head. 'I said it because I meant it. I always mean what I say.'

'How very annoying of you.' Laurel couldn't resist the soft jibe.

'True. But at least you'll always know where you stand,' Gideon pointed out. Hesitated. Then said softly, 'For when we're married.'

Laurel's heart stalled, then fluttered. She caught her breath. 'Oh. We're getting married, are we?' she managed to croak.

'I don't know,' Gideon said exasperated. 'Why ask me? You're the one who should know whether we're going to get married or not. You know everything else!'

'Oh. In that case, then we are,' she said firmly.

Gideon nodded. 'Right.'

He paused awkwardly. 'So that's sorted out. Now, about the chalice. You think we should go and confront Dr Ollenbach?'

Laurel nonchalantly scratched her chin. 'I think so. Don't you.'

Gideon nodded.

They left the room, walking without speaking to the car park where they climbed into the Morgan. Gideon pushed the key in the ignition and turned to her.

'We did just agree to get married, right?' he said.

'Right.'

'Just checking.'

Dr Felicity Ollenbach watched her husband drive away, an anxious look on her face. At the back of her mind she wondered, traitorously but realistically, if she'd ever see him again. He had, after all, a chalice worth a hundred thousand pounds with him.

He could just go off into the sunset with it, especially if he had a current mistress that he fancied himself in love with. Or if he convinced himself the bohemian wife-free life was the answer to all his problems.

She sighed and told herself not to get maudlin. She turned and shut the door and wandered into the kitchen. Make a sandwich? But the thought of food nauseated her. She paced some more, put on a CD, listened for a while, then turned it off. Paced some more.

The doorbell rang, making her jump.

Surely that wasn't Brian. Back because he'd forgotten something. But what? She flung open the door, and felt the colour drain from her face as first Gideon Welles and then Laurel Van Gilder, stepped firmly inside.

'It's not convenient,' Felicity heard herself saying, her voice as lacking in authority as she had ever heard it in her life.

'We know you have the chalice, Dr Ollenbach,' Laurel said firmly but gently, turning to face her, her eyes level.

'If you'll just hand it over, no more need be said,' Gideon added gently. 'Our Principal won't wish to take the matter further, I can assure you. And, at the moment, no one even knows it's missing.'

Felicity felt herself wilting, and just managed to get into a chair before collapsing. She shook her head helplessly.

'I can't help you,' she said flatly.

'It's already gone?' Laurel said sharply. 'When?'

'Just n…' Felicity closed her mouth with a snap. 'I don't know what you're talking about,' she finally found some backbone, but it felt precarious. As if it were made of matchsticks.

'"Just now", you were going to say, weren't you?'

Laurel predicted. 'Who's got it? Oh, your husband has it, of course,' she answered her own question, looking at Gideon helplessly.

'Who's agreed to buy it, Dr Ollenbach?' Gideon pressed. 'Francis Daye?'

Felicity jerked in surprise. She couldn't help it. How did they know?

Laurel nodded. 'Spot on. Come on, let's go. Dene the next stop.'

'It'll do you no good,' Felicity said rising unsteadily from the chair and staring at them defiantly.

'Oh, I think it will,' Gideon said, but not without pity. The poor woman looked at the end of her tether. 'From time-to-time, the Oxford colleges sell off a fair few of their treasures to collectors just like Mr Daye. If his name should be put on a blacklist, he won't like that at all. I think, to avoid such a thing, he'd be more than willing to hand over one little item.'

'Besides, Lord St John James is a man with a lot of clout in this town,' Laurel said frankly. 'I can't see Mr Daye being anxious to cross him.'

Dr Ollenbach's eyes flickered and brightened suspiciously. Gideon, sensing she was about to cry, looked away helplessly. After all, there was nothing he could do for her.

'Come on Gideon, let's go,' Laurel said softly and reached for the door. Gideon shut it gently behind them.

For a long moment, Dr Ollenbach simply stared at the door, her gaze unfocused. So that was it. It was over.

She was moving before she was aware of it and then had her handbag in her hand. What for? Oh of course. Brian.

She had to tell Brian. She reached for her mobile and dialled his mobile number.

On the second ring, Brian answered it.

'So, how far is it?' Laurel asked as they headed north-west out of Oxford and were quickly zooming along the main Oxford to Banbury road.

'About forty minutes away,' Gideon guessed vaguely. It was almost totally dark now, the sun having set and leaving only a dark-orange glow of light low on the horizon. He blinked as an oncoming car, forgetting to dip its main headlights, momentarily dazzled him.

'How far ahead of us do you think he is?' Laurel asked.

'Impossible to say. I only hope Mr Daye pays by cheque. That way he can always cancel it when he gives us the chalice back. If he's already paid Brian by cash, it'll be harder to persuade him to hand it over.'

Laurel grinned. 'Oh, he'll hand it over all right,' she said ominously.

Gideon glanced across at her, at her out-thrust chin and frowning dark brows, and felt a rush of tenderness wash over him. Strange, when she was looking as fierce and dangerous as a tigress returning to her den to find someone messing with her cubs.

'Cold?' he asked, turning up the heater when he noticed that she was shivering slightly.

She laid her head against the top of his arm and said softly, 'How many children do you want?'

Gideon nearly steered them into the hedge!

Once back on the straight-and-narrow, he laughed. 'I don't know. One of each?'

'Think they'll come along that obligingly?' she chuckled. 'What if we try and try and only have girls. All of them just like me.'

Gideon nearly steered them into a ditch!

He laughed almost helplessly. 'I don't know. I'll

run away and join a monastery.'

'Of course we could have all boys. All brainy like you. In which case, I'll buy up Bloomingdale's and move in.'

'Glad to know you've got your priorities right.'

'I like to think so.'

He turned the Morgan off the main road and soon they were on a tiny, winding, narrow lane.

The hedges grew so close to the sides, Laurel was sure they'd soon start scraping the paintwork.

A full moon had risen, bathing the countryside in a magical silver light. Away to their left, Laurel could see, in the ambient light, wave after wave of fields and hedges and trees.

'I'll bet there's some view along here in the daylight,' she said softly. 'Do you want to buy a house up this way?'

'I don't know. Do you want, specifically, to live in England?' he asked. Then added thoughtfully, 'Can you? Being the head of the whole shooting match, I mean.'

Laurel frowned. For the first time since his proposal, she came face-to-face with the brick wall that was the reality of her life. As the Van Gilder heiress.

'You know,' she said sadly, 'I don't think I can.' She felt her hand tightening instinctively on his arm and forced her grip to relax. But the truth was, she'd never felt more in danger. Or as scared.

'Gideon, do you think you could live in Boston?' she asked, holding her breath as she waited to find out whether her whole life would be miserable or happy.

'Oh, easily, I should think,' Gideon said with barely a moment's hesitation.

Laurel closed her eyes then opened them again, the air whooshing out of her lungs in a relieved rush. 'Oh Gideon,' she said softly, her voice choked with tears of gratitude and love.

Then her eyes widened. 'Gideon!' she shrieked again, only this time in fear.

For, lurching out of nowhere it seemed, was a big hefty Range Rover.

In fact, it was coming from a gap in the hedge where Brian Westlake had parked, lying in wait.

Brian had been nearly in Dene itself when his phone had rung. Cursing, he'd answered it, only to find out the bad news from Felicity.

The tall blond geek and the American princess had found them out. He'd pulled on to the side of the road and quizzed his wife mercilessly.

She'd tried to talk him into coming back, to hand over the chalice, to return to the *status quo*. But although he'd automatically soothed her, promising to come home and sort it out, his mind had been racing.

No way was he was going to give up the chalice. Why the hell should he?

He reversed, turned around and started to head back to Oxford, his mind whirling and his whole being seething with resentment. To be so close, only to have the prize about to be snatched away was more than he could bear.

He'd spotted a gap in the hedge, a break where the farmer had left access to his field of winter wheat, and pulled over to think.

It was while he was sat there, invisible to any passing cars, that he suddenly realised what he could do.

Gideon Welles drove a Morgan – a low-slung, old, flimsy sports car – and he was parked in a perfect place of ambush in a very solid Range Rover. It had air-bags, seat-belts, an iron-grid bumper.

He wasn't, consciously, thinking of killing them. Just scaring them. Perhaps roughing them up a little bit – putting them in hospital long enough for him to sell the chalice to the collector. After all, they could hardly threaten to put Francis Daye on anyone's hit-list if they were both in traction at the hospital, could they?

And so he'd waited. His palms sweating, his eyes aching as they scoured the night for a set of headlights.

Twice he'd seen them, only to realise it wasn't the right car – a small Datsun with an old woman at the wheel came first, and then a Volvo estate with a mother, two kids and a golden retriever that grinned at him from the back window.

It had felt as if they were never going to come. Minutes passed like hours. But then he'd heard the unmistakable roar of a sports car – a low, throaty growl. And the approach of headlights, so low to the ground it had to be the Morgan.

He'd turned on the engine, looking straight across the road. There was a tiny grass verge, then a ditch, hedged by a row of hawthorn and elder. All he had to do was ram them from the side and they'd be in the ditch. Perhaps roll over once or twice. Just enough to break some bones and keep them out of the picture.

He'd even call an ambulance from the village of Dene, after he'd done his business with the collector.

The dark green Morgan showed up as almost black in his lights as he shot forward, rocking a little in the seat from the force of his acceleration.

Gideon, in the Morgan, heard Laurel's screech of fear and warning, and then saw the whole of the left side of his peripheral vision fill with light.

Any other man would have instinctively rammed on the brakes. But Gideon's mind was already racing.

To brake now would be madness – it would slow them down and make them an even easier target to hit. Already his subconscious mind told him that it was Brian Westlake in the Range Rover, and that this was no ordinary traffic accident in the making.

'Hold on!' he yelled and rammed his foot on the accelerator. He'd been driving the car for years and knew exactly what it was capable of – the power under its hood and the state of the engine. He'd always kept the car perfectly maintained, and knew it wouldn't let them down.

Nor did it.

It surged and leapt forward, like a panther about to pounce. Laurel felt herself being pushed by the G-forces back against her seat, her head whipping back against the backrest.

Brian Westlake swore as the car seemed to fly past and pressed further on his own accelerator. He braced himself for impact, but the bulk of the car was already gone by the time his Range Rover had lurched far enough forward.

But the Morgan had not gone quite far enough. Brian's Range Rover hit the back rear fender and, in the Morgan, Gideon felt the car begin to skid, the road ahead becoming a kaleidoscope of tarmac, hedge, Range Rover, hedge and grass verge, as the car began to spin.

Laurel gripped on to the side of her door with fingers of iron, her teeth gritted determinedly together, forcing herself not to scream or cry out, or in any other way distract Gideon.

She, too, understood only too well who was in the Range Rover and what he was trying to do. She felt icy cold and could hear the roar of blood in her ears and feel the hot bite of fear grab her innards.

Gideon turned into the curve, his hands scissoring on the big steering wheel, concentrating too hard on keeping them on the road to be truly scared, although he was bitterly aware of a metallic taste filling his mouth.

The Morgan's wheels screeched and the smell of burning rubber filled the air, but the car never left the road. He eased on the brakes, slowing them.

Laurel felt the first sickening wave of fear leave her as she realised they weren't going to crash. Only now, the Morgan had turned a full circle and a half, and was facing the Range Rover.

Brian, who'd only just saved himself from going into the ditch by ramming on the brakes and turning hard, saw his opportunity and slammed the big vehicle into gear.

'Gideon, he's coming!' Laurel cried. 'Turn around!'

But Gideon saw at once he didn't have time to turn around. If he tried it, he'd once more be presenting the Morgan's vulnerable flank to the crushing bars of the Range Rover. Instead, he slammed the car into reverse and, twisting his body around to look out of the back window, began reversing.

Fast.

Very fast.

For a moment, Laurel closed her eyes, but then forced herself to open them.

Gideon had already created a large gap between them.

Brian Westlake, losing a few precious moments to blank surprise, stared at the fast-disappearing Morgan's headlights and then shot off in pursuit.

Gideon angled the car around a sharp bend, then another.

'He's gaining,' Laurel warned quietly, trying to keep her voice even and unworried.

'I know. We can't keep this up forever…hold on!' he yelled and, suddenly, they seemed to almost fall backwards. In reality, Gideon had spotted another gap in the hedge, this time on the right, and the path down into the field was a rutted and steep one. Brian Westlake overshot them and Laurel saw the night turn red as he slammed on his brakes, and the brake lights shone through the bare wintry hedge.

'He's coming back,' she said flatly and this time it was Westlake's turn to drive backwards.

Gideon slammed into first gear and revved hard – too hard. The wheels spun fruitlessly on the stony, muddy ground.

He forced himself to lower the revs, to move slowly and, only then, at the very last moment when they finally had hard tarmac beneath them, he shot forward.

As he shot out the gap, the rear of the Range Rover loomed over them, but once again the nifty, crafty, courageous little sports car had the edge and shot from beneath its bulk.

There was a grinding, scraping sound as the Range Rover hit the hedge. 'He's in the ditch,' Laurel crowed, then scowled as the off-the-road vehicle showed its own class and managed to power its way out.

'Oh no,' she cried.

But Gideon was away – pushing the speedometer and putting yards between them.

'The man's insane,' he growled. 'If we meet any traffic on this one-track lane going at speeds like this…' he said as he glanced at his speedometer, his eyes scouring the road ahead. 'We've got to…'

'He's not far behind us,' Laurel warned, staring over her shoulder.

Gideon grunted, saw a U-bend up ahead and hissed softly. 'Yes!'

He shot around the bend and then turned the car into a controlled spin. At the same time, he turned off his headlights then idled forward.

Laurel could hear the Range Rover's engine just ahead and could see the sweep of its headlights sweeping out across the field as it approached the bend.

But she never, for one moment, doubted that Gideon knew what he was doing.

Not even when one part of shock-numbed brain warned her that she was – literally – putting her life in his hands, did she ask him what he was doing. Or try to scramble out of the car.

And why should she? Another calm, accepting little voice piped up in the back of her head.

Just suppose for a moment that Gideon had got it wrong and she did abandon him by throwing herself out of the passenger door and rolling into a ditch. What good would life do her, if she then had to watch the Range Rover plough into the Morgan and kill the only man she'd ever loved? Or would ever love?

What use was her life without Gideon?

All these thoughts passed through her mind in less than seconds, and then suddenly Gideon was moving.

Hitting the lights on full-beam, they shot forward.

She took a breath – not caring if it was her last, so long as it was her last with Gideon.

In the Range Rover, Brian Westlake threw his hands up to his eyes as the dazzling light hit them, hurting him. Losing track of the road, the big vehicle lurched, first left, then as he tried to overcompensate, right.

Into the hedge.

In the Morgan, Gideon had to wait hideously long seconds, to see which way the big vehicle was going to go, before committing himself and the Morgan.

He slammed the wheel around just in time, and the Range Rover scraped the passenger side of the door as the two cars passed, the horrendous screech of metal-on-metal filling the night air.

Then the Morgan was on the grass verge, nearly toppling over into the ditch that side, but Gideon turned back into the road and pulled over, finally beginning to shake.

They both heard the screech of tortured metal and a crumpled, ominous bang, and Gideon turned off the engine, his hands cold and shaking.

'Wait here,' he told her curtly and, for the first time in her life, Laurel obeyed him.

He got out of the car and jogged back. The first thing he saw was the gap in the hedge, then the Range Rover lying on its side in a ploughed field.

He almost turned his ankle on the rough sod as he ran to get to the car, then he was on his knees looking inside. But Brian Westlake wasn't visible – only a large white air-bag.

'Brian!' he yelled. 'Brian, can you hear me? Can you speak?'

But there was only an ominous silence. Cursing, Gideon climbed to the top of the vehicle and wrenched opened the door, reaching inside. He felt material, managed to locate one arm and worked his way down to a wrist.

There was a pulse. Strong and steady.

As he lifted his arm, his elbow hit something hard and he yelped. Whatever it was (and it felt like a small hard suitcase), it was trapping his arm between it and the dashboard, so he rocked it loose and brought it back out of the Range Rover with him.

He slithered back on to the ground and trotted back on to the road, then ran to the Morgan.

Inside, he saw that Laurel was already on her mobile phone. As he opened the door, he heard her giving their location – presumably to the police or ambulance service. He opened the passenger door and stooped to look inside.

When she hung up she turned big, wide eyes on him. Her face looked ghostly pale in the moonlight.

'Is he OK?' she whispered.

'He's got a pulse,' he said quickly. 'How long before they get here?'

'They didn't say. Where will the ambulance have to come from?'

'I don't know,' he said blankly.

'What's in there?' Laurel asked and, it was only when she pointed downwards to his hand, that he realised he was still clutching the box. It was, he saw now, a big black square box with a gold clasp. The kind of travelling jewellery box that had been popular back in the twenties.

'I don't know,' he said again. 'It was in my way.' He slung it carelessly into the space between the wheel well, then felt his knees finally giving way.

He went down in front of her and, with a wordless cry, she swung her legs out and then pulled him close, cradling his head against her breast. Her hands ran through his hair, her fingertips pressing and massaging comfortingly against his warm scalp.

'It's all right,' she murmured, feeling his big body shake.

'I thought I might lose you,' he said, his voice muffled. 'No, worse than that. That I might be the cause of your death. Again. I'm going to sell this stupid car,' he said, pulling his head back and looking at her with agonised eyes. 'Twice it's almost killed you.'

In the moonlight, he looked more of an iceman than ever – his face pale, his hair silver, the glitter of his eyes almost silver.

'Oh no you won't,' she said, running her hand along

the doorframe and patting the car's framework lovingly.

'This Morgan is gonna be ours forever. She saved our lives tonight, remember?'

Gideon shuddered, then leaned forward again. He closed his eyes.

In the distance, they could hear the sound of sirens.

The police took their statements which, by common consent, they'd already agreed to keep as simple as possible. They'd been coming back from the direction of Dene when the Range Rover, travelling much to fast, had banged into them and then catapulted into the hedge.

They doubted, when he came around in hospital, that Brian Westlake would say anything different.

The ambulance staff who'd come and gone had been optimistic – they'd detected a fractured collarbone and a broken leg but not, they thought, any serious internal or head injuries. The air-bags had done their job well. Brian, they'd said, had been lucky.

Once it was over, Gideon insisted on driving back but slow and easy this time.

The Morgan, apart from the dents and affronts to her paintwork, purred like a well-satisfied cat after a particularly interesting night on the tiles.

It wasn't until they'd got back to Laurel's villa and had remembered the jewellery box, that Laurel pulled it up on her knees and opened it.

And found inside, undamaged and glowing serenely in the moonlight, the Augentine chalice.

They trooped inside, feeling bone weary and yet strangely alive. Gideon, at least, recognised the feeling as a combination of shock at their near brush with death, and euphoria at beating the grim reaper.

In the villa's spacious living room, Laurel shrugged off her shoes and coat and then stood staring down at the chalice in her hands. So much trouble for such a little thing. Still, she knew she'd always have a soft spot in her heart for this little silver cup.

It had brought her to England. To the lovely city of Oxford…and the man of her dreams.

'Do you have a safe?' Gideon asked, watching her place the precious silver object carefully down on to the coffee table in front of the sofa and giving it – of all things – an affectionate little pat.

'I don't think so. Why?' she asked curiously.

Gideon laughed. 'Just wondering. It would be a terrible thing if we had a normal burglar come tip-toeing in during the middle of the night and having the thing nicked again,' he pointed out drolly.

'Don't even think it!' Laurel screeched, giving him a mock thump on the top of his arm. 'That's not even funny.'

'Ouch!' Gideon said and rubbed his arm playfully. Then he sighed and ran a hand through his silvery hair. 'I suppose we could always take it up to bed with us. Sleep with it under the pillow,' he mused half-heartedly.

'What? And put a dent in it,' Laurel huffed. 'Not on your life, buster. Besides,' she trailed off, looking at him archly, 'what makes you think we're gonna spend the night together in the same bed? Did you hear me issue an invitation?'

Gideon glanced at her quickly to see if she was kidding, saw that she was and heaved a sigh of relief and then began to grin. 'Bit late in the day to start getting coy now, isn't it?' he teased her. 'Besides, if we're going to be a respectable married couple, we get to go to bed together whenever we feel like it, all nice and legitimate.

Even the most staid bachelor in St Bedes allows that married couples, if they really have to do that sort of thing, can share a bedroom in perfect rectitude. So long as we each keep one foot on the floor at all times of course,' he added, as he saw her wrinkle her nose at him playfully.

'I might even take my clothes off in front of you, if you're lucky,' he added magnanimously.

'Well, you romantic old fool you!' Laurel admonished. 'But you've got me curious. Which foot is it, exactly, that we have to keep on the floor at all times?'

'One right and one left, of course,' he grinned.

Laurel laughed. 'I take it these respective feet have to be on opposite sides of the bed?'

'Naturally. Or else…' Gideon blinked as he pictured in his mind the exact circumstances needed for both of their feet to be on the same side of the bed – his right, her left. Or vice versa. He was adaptable.

'Oh no. I'm sure that wasn't what they had in mind at all,' he laughed, backing away as she advanced menacingly on him.

'No?' she queried, her voice rising in a squeak of mock surprise. 'Pity that, because it's precisely what I had in mind. Come here. Grrr.' She made a sudden lunge for him and succeeded in tackling him down on to the sofa. The springs gave a surprised yelp that almost matched Gideon's.

Her lips came down and nibbled his ear lobe.

'The chalice,' he gulped, pointing at it feebly.

Laurel told him, in a few choice words, exactly what he could do with the chalice.

Gideon pointed out, reasonably enough, that it simply wasn't physically possible.

'No, but this is,' she said huskily, reaching her hand

down between them and rubbing her palm suggestively against the hardness that pressed against her there.

Gideon closed his eyes, his face taut. She watched his eyes flutter open and the smoky, fiery depths of his blue knowing gaze had her nipples hardening to attention.

'You keep on doing that,' he warned her huskily, 'and you're going to be in trouble, missy.'

'Promises, promises,' she whispered drolly, lowering her head and kissing him. Thoroughly. When she lifted her head at last, he drew in a deep, ragged gasp.

'We really need to talk,' he said but Laurel, who was busy undressing him, was too distracted to pay him much attention.

'Really? What about?' she asked vaguely. Then her voice became arch. 'You know, it amazes me how you academics can talk and talk and talk, even at the most inappropriate of times. Can't you see that I'm busy seducing you, man? Now shut up and let me get on with it.'

'You're a one to talk about talking,' he gasped, his big body shuddering as she found naked skin and dipped her head to take advantage of it.

He closed his eyes again as her hot mouth brushed against the sensitive skin above his ribs, and he jerked on the sofa, almost dislodging her. But she clung on hard.

'We still,' he panted, 'have to,' he gulped, 't-talk,' he gasped, as her hands found his belt buckle and began to unfasten it.

'Oh for Pete's sake!' Laurel said, her voice necessarily muffled, for she was now in the process of burrowing her tongue into his ear. 'What about?'

'Us,' Gideon groaned. 'The future.'

Laurel pushed her hands further down the front of his trousers, cupping and caressing, and Gideon arched, this time succeeding in getting his elbows under him. Then he managed to wriggle his way up into a near-sitting position, and lay back against the sofa arm panting.

When she looked at him, it was to see hectic colour on his cheekbones and a febrile light in his eyes.

'Men,' Laurel said disgustedly and settled herself more comfortably over him, until she had a knee on either side of his hip and was sitting snugly in his lap.

She was gratified to feel just how hard and lumpy his lap was. She wriggled her hips suggestively. 'So talk,' she said, faking a bored yawn and knowing, with smug feminine satisfaction, that at that precise moment in time, he simply didn't have any breath left to talk with.

'Talk? What about?' Gideon murmured at last, reaching for her and managing, in one supple motion, to slide his hands under her sweater and place one palm directly over each of her breasts.

Laurel gasped. 'Well I like that! Of all the sneaky, low-down tricks. I thought you were the one who was all in a lather about getting our future straightened out?' she accused.

She loved this. This playful, sexy, uninhibited side of him. If this was what he was like after only a few weeks, what kind of lover would she have after a couple of years?

'I am,' he said distractedly, watching the movement of his knuckles through the sweater as he massaged her breasts. 'In a lather, I mean. To talk.'

'Gideon.'

'What?'

'Are you going to make love to me or what?'

'What do you call this?'

'Aggravating,' she gasped and reached up to pull the sweater over her head, and then reached behind her to competently unhook the bra.

Gideon leaned forward to kiss the tender valley between her breasts and breathe in her scent.

'I love you,' he said softly.

Laurel closed her eyes, afraid that the tears might escape if she didn't, and tenderly brushed his hair from off his damp forehead.

'Thank you,' she said softly. 'I love you too.'

'And we're really getting married, right?' he said, his fingers walking down her hips to tug on the back of her skirt in silent command.

Obediently, Laurel unclasped it and let him push the garment down to slither across his lap.

'That seemed to be the general idea, as I remember it,' she agreed, as he tugged on the elastic of her panties suggestively. 'Anything else you need to know? Or can we ravish each other now?'

'Nope. There's one other thing. A pre-nup,' he said and Laurel immediately froze.

He felt her shock immediately.

'What?' she said, her voice faint and all sense of fun totally gone.

'A pre-nup,' Gideon repeated, lifting his eyes to look at her calmly. 'I know you tend to think of us Oxford Dons as mole-like creatures who live on cloud nine, or in some Victorian-like time capsule, but some of us do poke our heads out occasionally now and then to sniff the real air and breathe in some twenty-first century culture. So I do know what a "pre-nup" is.'

Laurel swallowed hard. 'Now you tell me.'

But in spite of her feeble attempt to get back to the sexy playful mood of just a few moments ago, in the back of her mind, warning bells were going off loud and clear.

In spite of herself, she remembered her first infatuation. (She could no longer call him her first love – knowing now what true love really meant.)

He'd wanted nothing from her but her money. Luckily though, she'd had her family to look out for her on that occasion.

But now here was Gideon, at the height of their passion, talking money.

She didn't like it. Not one little bit.

'You want to do without one, I suppose?' she said hollowly. 'Like it's some kind of a test for me? If I really love you, I'll marry you without any legal protection because we're never going to divorce so why worry about it? Is that it?' she asked, her voice a little hard. A little hurt.

A strange look crossed over Gideon's face. He became suddenly very still.

'And you would do that?' he asked quietly. It felt, for some reason, as if his life depended on her answer. Probably because it did.

Laurel stared down at him and the whole of her life – her life with Gideon – flashed across her mind.

The way she'd turned her bike into his Morgan and then woke up to see his face in hospital.

Their arguments.

Their love-making.

Their combined brush with death only a few hours ago.

The way he'd changed her whole life around.

When she'd first come to Oxford, she'd been a sad little princess mourning for her father and still, absurdly, totally unaware of what life was really all about.

Now she had a man to love and to marry. To have children with and grow old with. To die with, when the time came.

And for all of this, all he was asking in return was for

her to trust him.

Was it really so hard to do?

Everything about her past life said yes. All her family, as far as she knew, had married with air-tight pre-ups firmly in the bag. Her rich friends all did the same – it was just a sad, simple reflection of the way the seriously wealthy lived their lives. Always prepared to believe that somebody was out to con them.

Those who married poor, those who married for love, those who married in haste only to repent at leisure, were objects of pity or worse – scorned – by her crowd.

But that was her past life.

This was her life now.

She looked down into his face – his strong, fair, handsome face and met his level blue gaze.

'Yes,' she heard her voice saying. 'Yes, I'll marry you without a pre-nup. I'd marry you tomorrow. In a tent. Anything you say, sweetheart.'

Gideon reached up and put a finger to her lips. 'Enough,' he said softly. And the last piece of ice surrounding the iceman's heart finally melted.

'Now, if you'll let me get a word in edgeways and say what I was going to say before you interrupted me,' he told her, eyes twinkling. 'About this pre-nup thing. I want you to get one arranged. Talk to your solicitor. Whatever you and he think is fair, I'll sign it. Because, as far as I'm concerned, it'll never see the light of day again after that.'

Laurel gaped at him and didn't know whether to hit him or kiss him.

'Gideon!' she finally yelped. 'You could have saved me all that soul-searching and just said so right away!'

She felt as if she could cheerfully throttle him. Or love him to death. 'Besides, I don't know if I want a pre-nup now,' she said, knowing she sounded petulant and childish but not caring. 'Why do you want one anyway?' she demanded curiously.

'Because I'm not a gold-digger,' he said simply. 'I don't want you to keep me in a lifestyle that I could become accustomed to. I just want us to live together as equals. Partners. You can be the rich one, I'll be the clever one.'

Laurel grinned. 'Gee, thanks. I can be the pretty one, you can be the ugly one.'

'I can be the Nobel prize-winning one, and you can be the clothes horse.'

'I can be the first woman billionaire, and you can go suck eggs.'

'Grandmothers suck eggs, not Oxford Dons,' he corrected her pedantically.

'Ex-Oxford Don,' she corrected him primly. 'You're giving all this up to come and live with me in the lap of decadent luxury in the States, remember?'

But then a shadow crossed her face and she became pensive again. 'Gideon, all this larking about aside, you are sure, aren't you? I mean, really sure? About everything. It's such a big step to take.'

Gideon tugged her panties down and watched her face become tight and hot. 'Oh yes, I'm sure,' he said firmly. 'You know, you really do have the damnedest sense of timing,' he muttered. 'Wanting to chat instead of make love.' And so saying, he wriggled down beneath her, pulling off her panties as he did so. 'I thought you were supposed to be seducing me?' he complained.

'Oh, I was, I was,' she huffed, grunting a little in the effort of pulling down his trousers. He obliged by lifting his hips off the sofa.

'Well, if you don't mind my saying so,' he muttered, 'you don't seem to be making a very good job of it.'

Then he gasped as she suddenly sat down on him, trapping him inside her.

'Oh no?' she said, clenching her inner muscles and grinning wickedly.

Gideon sighed. 'Are you always going to want the last word?' he asked long-sufferingly, then moaned. 'Oh, yes, do that again.'

So Laurel did.

That night they slept upstairs entwined in each other's arms, totally forgetting about the chalice which stayed downstairs on the coffee table.

Luckily, it was still there when they got up again the next morning.

Laurel blamed Gideon for forgetting about it.

Gideon took it like a man.

chapter thirteen

It was Christmas Eve.

Laurel Van Gilder awoke and the moment she opened her eyes, she was alert, aware, excited.

This was her wedding day!

She got up, aware of a strange quality of quietness all around her. Puzzled, she walked to the window which was frosted over and flung it open, drawing in a gasp of surprise.

Snow!

It must have snowed persistently during the night, for now Oxford was layered in tiers of white. On the bare branches of the trees, on the road, on the gardens and houses and roofs. On the domes and pergolas and crenellated walls of the colleges.

Snow everywhere!

It was barely eight o'clock and, over in the east, the rising sun was casting a warm orange glow in contrast with the wintry scene.

Laurel caught her breath again at the sheer beauty of the spectacle, as Oxford's many snow-covered dreaming spires, domes, turrets and towers, began to glow orange as if someone had iced the city like a cake.

Everywhere she looked, layers of snow clung to clock faces, shrubs, railings and drainpipes.

As if on cue, a bell-ringing group practising for the traditional midnight service, began to peal the bells in a nearby church.

Suddenly the morning rang with the sound of

celebratory bells. Although she knew better, she could easily imagine that those bells were ringing just for her and Gideon!

Back in Boston, she supposed without regret, they probably would have been but Laurel had wanted to get married in England.

In Oxford, to be exact.

And Gideon, who would have gone to Lapland to get married if she'd wanted, had arranged for them to be married in the Chapel at St Bedes.

Rex Jimson-Clarke had agreed to be their minister.

Laurel shivered in the freezing air, but was reluctant to move away from the winter wonderland outside her window.

In the next room, she could hear the sound of movements though, and realised that her mother was now awake too. She'd flown in to the UK the moment Laurel had telephoned her a month ago and told her that she'd met the man she was going to marry.

At first, Laurel had been a little nervous about how her mother and the rest of the family and Gideon would get on but, in the event, she'd had no reason to be.

Her mother had been bowled over by Gideon at first sight when they'd picked her up from Heathrow Airport.

A small, dark woman herself, Laurel's mother had been instantly struck by Gideon's height and fairness. She'd also been much impressed by his intellect and even more impressed by St Bedes.

Although he was not an American and not a businessman, she had to admit that he would probably do!

And when Laurel had told her that she wanted to have a Christmas wedding in Oxford, it was as if she had let loose a whirlwind!

Quickly getting over the disappointment of not having the wedding back home in Boston, she'd set to with a vengeance.

The phone lines across the Atlantic had buzzed for weeks. Valentino had been commissioned to fly in and make the wedding gown. Top chefs had been commissioned and flown in from France, Italy, and the States to cater for the wedding reception, which was to be held in Hall.

Her mother had also engaged the services of the top wedding planner on the East coast, a tall, painfully thin man with a nervous habit of giggling, and a finicky personality that quickly drove Laurel wild.

But not even he had been able to find fault with the huge, high-ceilinged impressive Hall, with its ancient wooden floorboards, highly-burnished wooden panels, impressive chandeliers, and imposing set of portraits of past Principals that hung on every wall.

He'd been equally dazzled by the centuries-old chapel, and had gone into raptures over its elegant simplicity and beautiful stained-glass windows.

Galvanised and inspired by the ancient college, he'd gone in for a vaguely Elizabethan wedding theme that suited everybody concerned.

Of course, her mother had insisted that they raid Aspreys and Harrods for silverware, dining ware, flowers, gifts, and the million and one things you needed in order to throw a proper wedding fit for an heiress!

Gideon, after one bemused session with the hyperactive, sartorially elegant wedding planner and over-the-moon mother-in-law, had backed off in goggle-eyed alarm and Laurel had done the same.

They'd laughingly (and cravenly), agreed to everything and anything her mother and the wedding planner wanted, their only contributions to the wedding and reception being the choice of venue.

Gideon had chosen the destination of their honeymoon, of course, opting for a nature reserve in the Seychelles. After the madness of the wedding arrangements, Laurel could understand why a deserted island had appealed to him!

And to her!

Lord St John James had been both delighted to turn St Bedes over to the wedding party and appalled at the thought of losing Gideon Welles.

For Gideon had told him that Michaelmas term was to be his last at Oxford.

Laurel sighed now and reluctantly shut the window on the snowy scene and jubilant bells, and walked to the bathroom to run her bath.

The ceremony was due to begin at one-thirty.

All her relatives had now flown in from the States, and were being housed in both St Bedes itself, and the Randolf Hotel. The older generation of Van Gilders, of course, were at the Randolf where the rooms were bigger and they had room service.

The younger members of her family, however, had preferred to live in the college rooms, be they ancient, sloping-floored, and utterly self-service.

It took Laurel back to her own student days, to visit her cousins in Webster or Walton, and gossip about this, that and the other.

The college itself had been transformed, both for the wedding, and for the Christmas season.

A huge Christmas tree stood in the main entrance way in Webster and wreaths of holly, ribbons, fir cones, and golden bells, hung on every door.

Gideon's room was bedecked with greenery and tinsel,

for Laurel loved this time of year which was why she'd chosen it as the date for her wedding.

Since their engagement, of course, she'd been practically living in Gideon's rooms anyway, and had been responsible for the decorating of the Christmas tree that Gideon had never used to bother with.

She'd only slept in the villa last night in order to observe the proprieties. And because, of course, she didn't want him to see her before the ceremony.

All around her, as she soaked luxuriously in the tub filled with gardenia bath salts, the day began to marshal itself into some sort of order.

Laurel's mother, in a state of high nerves, had decided to leave the last-minute detailing to the wedding planner and, even now, he was checking out the famous St Bedes' chapel, ensuring that all the flowers were arranged and placed correctly, strictly as ordered.

The cake had already arrived and was being guarded zealously by St Bedes' chef in the college kitchens, and vans carrying crates of champagne were already unloading in the college car park.

Laurel, idly lifting one leg to soap her calf, wondered tenderly what Gideon was doing.

With a sigh, she got out of the tub and began to dry herself.

Time was marching on.

As if reading her mind, her mother chose that moment to tap on the door and tell her that the hairdresser had arrived.

Laurel still found it hard to believe it was her wedding day!

And yet, it was already the most magical day of her life.

She dressed in gossamer-fine white silk underwear and

slipped on a dressing gown.

In less than an hour's time, she would be Mrs Gideon Welles.

In his room in St Bedes, Gideon too was dressing. His tailor had just helped him put on the grey silk jacket of his morning suit, and he was now busy brushing him down with a clothes brush. Gideon had hired him from Oxford's oldest bespoke tailors shop. His best man had arrived last night, an old friend of his from school-days, and when he tapped on the door and walked in looking chipper and innocent, Gideon grimaced at him good-naturedly.

The stag night his old friend had arranged for him last night had been one of the more outlandish affairs he'd ever been to.

When everyone had been well lubricated with whisky, a Strip-o-gram girl, dressed as a WPC, had arrived and nearly turned the pub on its head. So far, everybody was denying commissioning her!

Gideon returned to stand in front of the mirror and glanced at himself wryly. The silver grey morning suit did devastating things to his fair hair, and the bespoke tailoring fitted his long, lean length to utter perfection.

He accepted a red carnation from his tailor and fixed it in his buttonhole.

Philip, his best man, slapped him on the back. 'You sure you know what you're doing mate? That Laurel is a major package to have to handle.'

Gideon laughed. 'That Laurel is a big-mouthed, big-hearted, major pain in the neck!' he corrected.

He met his own blue gaze in the mirror. 'And I couldn't live another day without her,' he added so softly that Philip didn't catch it.

'Got the ring?' Gideon asked crisply, turning away from his reflection with a nod of determination. He felt a bit like an astronaut, about to go into space for the first time.

Elated and scared stiff at the same time!

Philip patted his pocket reassuringly. 'Right here. Don't worry – everything's under control.'

He himself had been married for four years and had moved away from Oxford a year before that. But he and Gideon had always stayed in touch, and he'd been delighted to be asked to be best man.

Gideon nodded and took a deep breath. They had only to walk across the gardens and quads to the chapel which was opposite the main lodge, and that would hardly take a minute.

They had plenty of time yet. He walked slowly to the window and looked out across the snow-spangled lawns.

Dr Ollenbach had resigned from her college and had returned to the United States only last week. He didn't think Brian had gone with her. He knew that the man had left the hospital after ten days, but that was all.

Neither he nor Laurel had felt vindictive, even if he had tried to run them off the road. They'd just been too happy, too caught up in themselves, to want to go through a court case.

Besides, they'd both felt profoundly sorry for Dr Felicity Ollenbach. As Laurel had said – they'd got the chalice back in one piece and avoided scandal for everyone concerned – and had found each other into the bargain.

That was enough for anyone. Why be mean and make another woman's life miserable?

Sin-Jun had been suitably grateful and impressed when they'd walked into his office the next day and presented it to him, but hadn't been surprised when he'd asked no questions.

So that was that.

This was now.

'It's hard to grasp the fact that this is my wedding day,' he said thoughtfully. 'There was a time when I never thought this day would ever come. That like Rex, or any other number of men I could mention, I would live out my life here into a sedate and dignified old age.'

He shook his head. Impossible to think now, how he could have regarded such a loveless, tame life, with such equanimity.

'No chance of that in America, mate,' his best man said cheerfully. 'I hear you're going into private practice over there?'

Gideon nodded. 'Yes, I am. Laurel's family is over there, and so is her work. I received an offer to teach at Harvard, but I think it's time I put my knowledge to some more practical use. To help people. I thought I'd find a practise and go into partnership. Perhaps specialise. Child psychology, maybe.'

'Well, there'll be no shortage of people over there who could use a good shrink,' his best man said prosaically. 'I can't say I envy you.'

But, in truth, Gideon was looking forward to it.

A new life beckoned. A new life with Laurel. What more could he ask?

In her house on the Woodstock Road, Laurel, helped by her mother and the two cousins who were her bridesmaids, stepped into her wedding dress.

It was a creation of white lace, silk and real pearls, and had a high lace neck and a heart-shaped panel of lace over the valley between her breasts that was just see-through enough to hint at the tops of her creamy breasts. It had a pinched in waist that tapered to a diamond panel, and then full, voluminous skirts underneath.

Her bouquet was comprised of orchids, flown in especially from Hawaii.

With her raven dark hair piled high on her head, and a string of pearls looped through the swirls of hair, she looked breathtaking.

A short, filmy veil did little to hide her radiant face.

A silver ghost Rolls Royce pulled up outside, ready to take her the short distance to the chapel.

Her mother was in tears.

At St Bedes, the guests were beginning to file into the chapel. Gideon came in a few minutes later and walked to the front.

The St Bedes' choir was assembled in the stalls, ready to sing the heartbreakingly lovely hymns that Laurel and Gideon had chosen.

Gideon stood facing the altar and feeling good. All traces of fear and uncertainty fell away.

He was about to marry the most wonderful, aggravating, beautiful, self-opinionated woman in the world. And she was just what he'd always needed.

Or would ever want.

As the organ began to play the Wedding March at last, everyone turned to watch the bride walking down the aisle.

She was so beautiful, the whole chapel seemed to make a collective gasp.

Gideon's eyes glowed like Ceylon sapphires, as far removed from ice as it was possible to get, as she moved towards him.

With her favourite uncle by her side, Laurel walked slowly towards the man she loved.

Gideon felt tears smart in his eyes and quickly blinked them back.

Outside, just as Laurel reached his side, it began to snow harder as if in honour of the iceman and his lady.

Heartline Books
Romance at its best

The Windrush Affairs *by Maxine Barry*	£3.99
Soul Whispers *by Julia Wild*	£3.99
Beguiled *by Kay Gregory*	£3.99
Red Hot Lover *by Lucy Merritt*	£3.99
Stay Very Close *by Angela Drake*	£3.99
Jack of Hearts *by Emma Carter*	£3.99
Destiny's Echo *by Julie Garrett*	£3.99
The Truth Game *by Margaret Callaghan*	£3.99
His Brother's Keeper *by Kathryn Bellamy*	£3.99
Never Say Goodbye *by Clare Tyler*	£3.99
Fire Storm *by Patricia Wilson*	£3.99
Altered Images *by Maxine Barry*	£3.99
Yesterday's Man *by Natalie Fox*	£3.99
Running for Cover *by Harriet Wilson*	£3.99
Moth to the Flame *by Maxine Barry*	£3.99
Second Time Around *by June Ann Monks*	£3.99
Secrets *by Julia Wild*	£3.99
Marrying a Stranger *by Sophie Jaye*	£3.99
Special Delivery *by June Ann Monks*	£3.99

Tell us what you think!

Because we want to make sure that we continue to offer you books which are up to the high standard you expect, we need to know a little more about *you* and your reading likes and dislikes. So please spare a few moments to fill in the questionnaire on the following pages and send it back to us.

Questionnaire

Please tick the boxes to indicate your answers:

1 Did you enjoy reading this Heartline book?

Title of book: ______________________________

A lot ☐
A little ☐
Not at all ☐

2 What did you particularly like about this book?

Title of book: ______________________________

Believable characters ☐
Easy to read ☐
Good value for money ☐
Enjoyable locations ☐
Interesting story ☐
Favourite author ☐
Modern setting ☐

3 If you didn't like this book, can you please tell us why?

____

____

4 What other kinds of books do you enjoy reading?

Puzzle books ☐
Crime/Detective fiction ☐
Non-fiction ☐

Other ______________________________

5 Which magazines and/or newspapers do you read regularly?

a) ____________________

b) ____________________

c) ____________________

d) ____________________

6 Our books can be ordered directly from us at www.heartlinebooks.com and we are always interested to know what you would like to see on our website:

a) Exclusive celebrity/author interviews?
Interested ☐ Not Interested ☐

b) Competitions, puzzles etc?
Interested ☐ Not Interested ☐

c) Special offers?
Interested ☐ Not Interested ☐

d) Readers' letters?
Interested ☐ Not Interested ☐

What else would you like to see on our website?

____

____

____

And now a bit about you:

Name ______________________________________

Address ____________________________________

____

____________________ Postcode ____________

We may use this information to send you offers from ourselves or selected companies, which may be of interest to you. If you prefer not to receive such offers, please tick this box ☐

Thank you so much for completing this questionnaire. Now just tear it out and send it in an envelope to:

HEARTLINE BOOKS
FREEPOST LON 16243
Swindon SN2 8LA

(If you don't want to spoil this book, please feel free to write to us at the above address with your comments and opinions.)

Heartline Books...

Romance at its best™